Praise for N. J. Walters' Discovering Dani

5 Blue Ribbons "Discovering Dani is very moving, sensual, and breathtaking. Ms. Walters knows how to pull her readers into her books. She tries to show us that her characters can be real and they also express emotions from the heart. This new series is bound to be her most beautiful work. I was taken away by Dani and Burke. Highly recommended."

~ Connie Spears, Romance Junkies

4 ½ Stars "Discovering Dani makes the reader believe they are actually a part of the story and not just reading it…I know that I cannot wait until the next installment of this series is released and N. J. Walters has my praise for writing a fantastic tale that involves not only the imagination but also your senses."

~ Sheryl, EcataRomance

5 Pink Hats Off Salute "…plenty of passion, topped with humor…The setting of this story will put your mind at ease for a sensuous read, pulling you in from page to page. I definitely suggest you move this book to the top of your list of reads."

~ TIC, The Pink Posse

"This book is remarkable. The characters flow, the scenes are smooth, and I just liked it. It goes without saying that N. J. Walters is an author I look forward to reading over and over again."

~ Talia Ricci, Joyfully Reviewed

"In Dani and Burke, N. J. Walters has created a couple that I truly loved, and following their bumpy relationship captivated me. DISCOVERING DANI will grab your attention from the beginning and leave you with a happy and satisfied smile by the end. This tale earns a place on my keeper shelf and has me keeping an eager eye out for Ms Walters's next book."

~ *Vicki Turner, Romance Reviews Today*

4 Red Hearts! "This is a beautiful, moving story and the start of a promising series…Ms Walters writes believable characters that reach into the reader's heart and pull on all the emotional strings…The reader will be drawn in on the first page and will almost hold her breath until the last. Sensuous and very romantic, Ms Walters knows exactly how to make her reader laugh and sigh…This reviewer can see this series being very successful and is looking forward to visiting Jamesville in the very near future."

~ *Valerie, Love Romances*

4 Angels "Discovering Dani is a wonderful story about overcoming tragedy and understanding the importance of family. Burke Black is a man that has had a very rough beginning in life. This has sculpted who he becomes as an adult. …The best person that could happen to him is Dani. Dani herself has had some difficult times in her life. …Her world resolves around family, something that Burke has never had. Together they pull the reader in with their sincerity, honesty and hopes for a love that can last an eternity. The passion between them is sweet yet intense. NJ Walters may find this change of pace novel bringing more fans her way. Definitely worth indulging in."

~ *Anita, Fallen Angel Reviews*

4.5 Magical Wands "This is a lovely, warm romance, the kind in which nothing and everything happens. …Dani is such a sympathetic woman, you'll find yourself caring about her from the moment you first meet her. Burke is smouldering and sexy with a painful past; and the supporting cast, especially Dani's brother, Patrick, are just wonderful. A great read."

~ Autiotalo, Enchanted Ramblings

4 ½ Roses "...N.J. Walters has proven herself time and again in the erotic romance genre, but in Discovering Dani she tones things down a bit and pens a beautiful sweet romance that is sure to satisfy fans and first time readers both."

~ Jackie, A Romance Review

4 Red Tattoos! "N. J. Walters has penned a heart warming tale built on the bedrock of any good romance story -- love, trust, and acceptance. ...This story focuses on Burke and Dani's developing love story. The sexual elements are just the icing on the cake, so to speak. I enjoyed reading Discovering Dani and I look forward to N. J. Walters next book."

~ Ophelia, Erotic Escapades

4 Cups of Coffee "This is a story of a city boy and a country girl, two worlds trying to weave together and find a middle ground where love can plant its seed and grow. ...The romance crafted here has a delicate touch and is rather endearing. It has the feel of a book you want to curl up with on a cold night, wrapped in a cozy blanket with a cup of hot cocoa to compliment the way the author's words warm your heart."

~ Charissa, Coffee Time Romance

Discovering Dani

by N. J. Walters

A Samhain Publishing, Ltd. publication

Samhain Publishing, Ltd.
PO Box 2206
Stow OH 44224

Discovering Dani
Copyright © 2006 by N. J. Walters
Cover by Scott Carpenter
Print ISBN: 1-59998-118-1
Digital ISBN: 1-59998-011-8
www.samhainpublishing.com

First Samhain Publishing, Ltd. electronic publication: March 2006
First Samhain Publishing, Ltd. print publication: June 2006

Discovering Dani

by N. J. Walters

Dedication

Thank you, Crissy, for taking a chance on publishing a book that was so different from anything else I've ever done.

Thank you, Ansley, for your enthusiasm and your hard work in helping to make this manuscript even better.

As always, thank you to my husband for his continued belief and support in whatever I do.

And thank you to my readers for allowing me to try new things and grow as a writer. You're the best!

Chapter One

"Don't just stand there, man, push!"

Dani O'Rourke flinched inwardly even as she stepped up to the beige Mercedes and placed her mitten-covered hands next to a large pair of leather-gloved hands on the cold, hard bumper. She shoved as hard as she could, while the car's wheels spun crazily in the slush.

"Harder!" the male voice growled.

Bracing her booted feet as best she could on the snow-covered ice, Dani pushed with all her might.

"Again!" the voice demanded. Once more, she threw her weight against the back of the car as it started to rock back and forth.

"Put some muscle into it," the male voice ordered.

One more shove sent the car spinning from the icy patch and a shower of cold snow spraying into her face. Dani sputtered and swiped at her face with her black wool mitten as she straightened up and watched the man who had issued the terse commands walk slowly toward the front of the car without a backward glance.

"Thank you ever so much," a girlish voice gushed from the driver's seat. "I don't know what I would have done if you hadn't stopped to help."

Sighing, Dani turned away and trudged down the road, unnoticed by either. She knew the car's owner, or more specifically, she knew *about* the car's owner. Everyone in Jamesville was familiar with Cynthia James and the James family. Her family's ancestors had settled the town a hundred years before and were still heavily involved in real estate and banking. Cynthia was beautiful and she knew it. She had the long blonde hair, blue-eyed, California girl appearance that men seemed to find irresistible. All she had to do was bat her eyelashes and smile, and men fell all over themselves to please her.

Dani pictured the stranger in her mind's eye, wondering who he was. Born and raised in Jamesville, she knew everyone, if not personally, then by sight. She suspected he was probably visiting friends or just passing through.

What does it matter to you? She scolded herself impatiently. A man like that would never notice a woman like her. Her hair was a plain medium brown that was usually worn in a no-nonsense braid that fell to her waist, and she'd never had the money or the inclination to wear makeup. Her few attempts at mascara and eyeliner had left her feeling more like a raccoon than a model. Somehow, she never felt quite right if she was wearing anything more than lip-gloss.

She could still picture his coal black hair, damp and shining from the falling snow. Eyes almost as black as his hair, snapping with impatience, as he'd issued his commands. An aura of power and arrogance had surrounded him as he'd barked his orders with no doubt that they would be followed.

Of course, she reasoned, he had the size to back it up. He was built like a mountain, tall and broad, with a face that looked as if it were carved from stone. A long jagged scar had bisected his left cheek. Dani thought it gave him the dangerous air of a pirate or a highwayman. *Just like the unsuspecting hero in a romance novel*, she mused.

"Stop it, Dani O'Rourke," she muttered as she reached her truck and dug into her pocket for her keys. "He thought you were a man, for heaven's sake." But she could understand why. At five-foot-eight, she was a tall woman and solidly built. Not overweight, but sturdy. Wearing her brother's hand-me-down parka that zipped around her face and covered her to her knees, well, it was no wonder he had mistaken her for a male. She consoled herself even as she wondered why the thought made her head hurt.

She had wasted enough time, lusting for things she could not have. There was work to do. It was the same lecture she had been scolding herself with for the past seven years, ever since her mother died and she became sole guardian of her brothers. If it sounded a little flat, well, that was just too bad, she told herself as she unlocked the door to her truck and prepared herself to face the rest of the day.

Burke glanced at the blonde-haired, blue-eyed beauty who smiled at him from the driver's seat of the luxury sedan. She flipped her hair back with a practiced motion and batted her eyelashes at him, sizing him up, as she offered her thanks yet again. Her good looks left him unmoved as the calculating look in her eyes, speculating his worth, was all too familiar.

"Thank you ever so much. I don't know what I would have done if you hadn't stopped to help. My name is Cynthia James. Are you new in town?"

Burke ignored her question and countered with one of his own. "What about the other guy? Aren't you going to thank him too?"

Cynthia's perfect smile grew wider and then she started to laugh. "That's really funny. You thought that was a guy helping you? Wait until I tell my friends. They'll love a good laugh."

Burke scowled, and she quickly lost her smile under his glare. "What do you mean?"

"That was Dani O'Rourke. *Miss* Dani O'Rourke. Don't worry about it though, I mean, it was only Dani. What did you say your name was?"

"My name is Black, Miss James. Have a nice day." He turned and limped away from the car and back to his four-wheel drive truck. His truck was new, but the trip here had covered it in road salt and dust, giving it well-earned character. He heard her call out to him, but didn't look back as he climbed into the cab.

As Burke settled himself into the driver's seat his left leg started to throb. Lost in thought, he absently rubbed it with his left hand as he turned the key in the ignition with his right. Even though it had been almost five months since the accident, he still was surprised when his body ached some days. He guessed the fourteen-hour days that he'd put in at the office since his release from hospital hadn't helped, but they had been necessary for his plans.

He glanced in the rearview mirror and the coal black eyes that stared back at him were as cold as the smile that he bestowed upon himself. He knew the scar that now bisected his left cheek from temple to chin, along with his dark as night hair, gave him a slightly demonic appearance. All in all, that knowledge pleased him. It suited his mood. Black.

His thoughts drifted back to those long weeks he'd spent lying in a hospital bed, after a drunk driver who'd sped through an intersection had hit his car. Other than the obligatory visits of business associates and doctors, he had spent it alone. He'd had too much time to think, and the conclusions he reached had left him in a dark temper.

Being confined to a wheelchair, even for a few weeks, had made him feel weak and helpless. His broken left leg, encased in a plaster cast from hip to thigh, had made him feel useless. He was unable to do for himself for the first time in his life, and he didn't like the feeling.

And oddly enough, he had felt lonely. That, too, had made him angry. He'd never relied on anyone in his life. He'd learned at a young age that to do so was a mistake. People looked out for themselves, and so did he. Still, there had been no one in his life, except for paid help, who would have been upset if he'd been killed in that accident. That felt wrong somehow. And that realization had changed him.

A genuine smile lit his lips as he remembered the conversation he had had with his second-in-command on his first day back at work. At first his Vice President, Jim Thomas, had refused to believe him when he had announced he was selling everything.

"Are you crazy, Burke?" Jim had had a stunned look on his face as he sank slowly into the padded leather seat behind him, as if his legs could not bear the shock of the announcement.

"No, Jim, I'm not. I'm thirty-five years old and I have more money than I could spend in my lifetime. Besides, I'm only selling off the company's business interests. I'll still have my own personal investments to keep me occupied."

"What in the name of God are you going to do with yourself? You'll be bored to death within a week. Think this through, Burke. Don't make any rash decisions that you'll regret later."

"Don't worry, Jim. I'll make sure you're taken care of." Burke was smart enough to realize Jim's concern was for his own position and not for his boss's health. After all, the only time Jim had shown up at the hospital was when business decisions needed to be made or when papers needed to be signed.

With the speed and ruthlessness that had made him a multimillionaire to begin with, he had sold everything. His business concerns, his large lavish home with the expensive furniture where he slept but didn't really live, and the foreign sports car that he drove back and forth to work. He relinquished all the trappings that had been associated with his old life, one by one. Gone were the designer suits, starched white shirts and silk ties, and in their place came blue jeans and cotton shirts.

Taking a deep breath, Burke looked away from the mirror and pulled his thoughts back to the present. Putting the truck in gear, he pulled away from the curb where it had been parked. He had forgotten how much he liked wearing jeans and driving a truck. These days he had no one to answer to but himself and that's what had brought him to the small community of Jamesville. A business associate had casually mentioned it as a good place to do some fishing. He might not be interested in the fishing, but it had exactly what he needed right now. Peace and quiet, and anonymity.

He was responsible for no one but himself, and no one wanted anything from him. God knows he had earned it. He'd been taking care of himself for as far back as he could remember. His mother, when she'd been sober, hated having a child to look after and had let him know at every moment how much he had ruined her life. He'd scrounged meals where he could get them and clothes from the local church charity. Anger and humiliation drove him to better himself. He'd studied hard and stayed out of her way. One sunny spring day, he came home to find their apartment empty. He'd found some of his belongings in the Dumpster out back.

At fifteen, he'd dropped out of school, lied about his age, and started in construction. He'd worked physically hard in the days and mentally hard at night. Eventually, he'd gotten his high school diploma at night school. Then he'd started taking business classes.

He invested in his first run-down building when he was twenty and got lucky when real estate values had soared in that section of Chicago five years later. By that time, he'd owned several buildings and had sold them for a huge profit and reinvested in more property. He had a knack for knowing which

15

property would increase in value, as well as the patience to wait. But after twenty years of non-stop work, he was filthy rich and very tired.

He pulled into the parking lot of the small grocery store he had passed the night before and parked the truck. "Greer's Grocery and Gas Bar" was printed with black letters on a white sign attached to the front of the building. He'd pick up a few things now and then head back to the cabin he had rented for the next few months and unpack his things. He was suddenly anxious to get settled in. Then he had to find a woman named Dani O'Rourke and apologize for this morning's slight misunderstanding.

Chapter Two

Dani stamped the snow off her boots as she let herself into Cozy Cabins rental number five. The first thing she saw was the pile of suitcases and boxes in the center of the living room floor. Obviously, the new tenant had checked in early. According to her schedule, he wasn't due until tomorrow.

"Hello, is anyone here?" Dani waited a couple of seconds by the front door for a reply. When only silence answered her, she picked up her supply box from the front porch and went inside. If the place was empty, she might as well clean it. Since the tenant hadn't unpacked, she could easily clean without disturbing their belongings. Dani unzipped her big navy parka and draped it over the back of the couch, picked up her cleaning supply box, and strode to the small kitchen at the back of the cabin.

As she placed her supplies on the counter, she noticed a black briefcase sitting on the kitchen table. The leather on the case looked expensive, and on closer inspection, she could see that the initials B. B. had been discreetly etched on a brass plate near one of the locks. This was obviously custom-made and not something one picked up at a local department store. Carefully,

17

she picked it up and placed it safely on the kitchen counter. That way she could clean the table and the floor around it and not have to worry about damaging the briefcase. That done, she set to work.

She sang along with the tune on the radio as she cleaned and disinfected the refrigerator. It was a country song about a man who felt he was too young to feel as old as he did. She laughed at herself. "Country singer I'm not." She enjoyed country music and although some days she related to the words of the music, today she felt pretty darn good. She loved the Cozy Cabins, as they represented her business beginnings.

She could still remember the first time she'd driven out here to clean them. Dani had only been eighteen years old when her mother died, and she'd quit school to look for work. Luckily, they'd already owned the little house they lived in.

She'd only been sixteen when her father had died of a heart attack and her mother had used a good portion of the life insurance policy to pay off the mortgage. Dani had spent the next two years after her father's death watching her mother just fade away. Her mother had not been the same after big Patrick O'Rourke had died.

Dani had taken over the running of the house and the care of her two younger brothers, Patrick Jr. and Shamus, but her mother's presence had enabled her to stay in school. When her mother passed away after a short battle with cancer, Dani discovered there wasn't enough money left to bury her. Her mother hadn't worked, and medical bills combined with just plain living had finished off what was left of the insurance

---

money. It had been scary for an eighteen-year-old to find herself responsible for two boys only nine and twelve years of age.

People had been kind to them and many had donated money so Dani hadn't had to get a loan to pay for the burial. After the funeral, well-meaning people had started talking about where the boys should be sent now that there was no one to take care of them. She'd been furious, and determination had filled her. They had lost too much already. They were a family, and no one was going to split them apart.

They had the house, but she knew she needed a steady income to prove to the authorities that she could take care of her brothers. She had placed notices all over town that she was willing to clean people's homes. At first, she had gotten little work, but then she'd come up with a new idea.

She'd approached the local real estate company with a business proposition, offering to clean the homes that were being listed by the Jamesville Real Estate Company. Most people, she reasoned, didn't want to clean a house they were moving out of, and most buyers wanted to move into a clean home. Mr. Carter, the owner of the Jamesville Real Estate Company, had listened to her proposition. He hadn't laughed at her or scoffed at her idea. Instead, he'd become her first corporate client.

"Miss O'Rourke," Mr. Carter had begun. "I believe you and I can do business." He had then helped her to set up her own small business enterprise and signed the first contract with O'Rourke Cleaning Services. He also signed a contract with her for cleaning the Cozy Cabins, which were a group of six vacation cabins he and his brother, Ernest, owned and rented.

The first cleaning job she had undertaken, as the proud new owner of her own business, had been Cozy Cabins number five. Heady stuff for an eighteen-year-old. The job had enabled her to keep her family together and to provide a future for her brothers. Once she had established herself as a legitimate business, other corporate clients had followed, including the Jamesville Bank and Dr. Parker's office. Now at twenty-five, she was proud of what she had accomplished. It felt good to be a respected member of the community.

Dumping the last bucket of dirty water down the sink, Dani turned and surveyed the kitchen with pride. The stove and refrigerator shone, and the counters and floors gleamed. She knew that the bathroom was spotless and crisp white linens hung from the towel racks. Fresh sheets were on the bed, and the furniture in the bedroom glowed with the combination of furniture polish, lemon oil, and elbow grease. The living room was ready for its new inhabitant to kick back and relax.

Dani rinsed the bucket and dried it with a rag, returning it to the small utility closet in the kitchen. Kicking the door closed with her foot, she dropped the rag into her own box. She ran tomorrow's schedule over in her mind as she checked to make sure she had all her supplies and tools packed. Satisfied she had everything she'd brought with her, she lowered the lid and snapped it shut.

She knew she had only one job tomorrow afternoon, but it would take almost the entire afternoon. That left only the morning free for her to run errands and to Christmas shop. Earlier this morning, she'd managed to find two sweaters on sale, one each, for Patrick and Shamus. Those packages were tucked away in the truck, but she wanted to look for new jeans for both her brothers. They wore them out quickly at their ages.

With her mind on her shopping, she picked up her belongings, swung around, and remembered the briefcase a fraction of a second too late. She dropped her own box and made a wild grab, but it was too late. She cringed as the case hit the floor, handle-side down, and popped open, strewing papers everywhere.

"Oh my, Lord," she gasped out, horrified that she might have damaged the briefcase and its contents. Dropping to her knees, Dani frantically started to gather the papers together. She was so focused on her task, she never heard the faint sound of the front door opening and closing.

"What the hell do you think you're doing?"

Dani had only a second to register the fury in the male voice before she was forcibly spun around and found herself trapped by eyes gone black with anger. She instinctively tried to pull away from the threat in those eyes, but the small movement seemed to anger him even more, and the grip on her wrist tightened.

"Oh, no you don't, sweetheart." The softness in his voice made her shiver, but there was no gentleness on the masculine face before her.

"Let...let me go," Dani stammered as she forced her voice to work.

"Oh, no you don't," he repeated. His grip on her arm was unbreakable as she again tried in vain to sever his hold on her. "If you're going to break and enter you should at least have had the sense to keep a better look-out."

Dani stared at the same mountain of arrogance she had run into earlier, and a sudden certainty filled her. He was the new tenant of cabin number five. It was the final straw in a day that had tested her temper. Taking a deep breath, she silently counted to five. It wouldn't do to yell at a client of her customer. Swallowing back her angry words, she summoned her best professional voice.

"I'm afraid there's been a mistake," Dani said through her clenched teeth. Her jaw ached with the strain of trying to contain the anger this man had provoked in her.

"You bet there's been a mistake. And you're the one who made it. No one steals from me." He dragged her relentlessly toward the phone, even as she dug in her feet and continued to fight his hold on her. "You can tell it to the police."

Burke glared down into the face of the woman he held, his irritation growing as his body ignored his mind and started responding to her as a woman. And what a woman she was. Long brown hair, the color of thick rich molasses, was working its way loose from its braid. Generous breasts and hips that would fit him quite nicely given her height. Most women didn't have curves like that these days as they all seemed intent on starving themselves. Stormy bluish-gray eyes shot daggers back at him as she parted her full pink lips.

Those lips were made for kissing, he thought, and then mentally shook himself. After all these years, he thought he was smart enough not to be swayed by a woman's looks. He knew what women were like, for God's sake. They'd use their feminine wiles if they figured it would get them out of trouble.

And who's to say it wouldn't? All of a sudden, he was curious to find out how far she would go.

"Are you suggesting I not call the police?" Burke waited patiently for her reply, sure that an offer was about to follow.

"Of course you shouldn't call the police. There's been a simple mistake which, if you'll just listen for one minute, I'll explain." She pulled away one more time and seemed surprised when he released her from his grip.

She straightened her sweater and tugged it down over her hips. The action outlined her breasts and hips in great detail. Burke watched her hands smooth down the front of her sweater and suddenly he wanted to do it for her. His temper flared again.

"Look, Mister..." she began.

"The name's Burke Black, and you can forget the coy explanations. I'll take what you're offering and I won't call the police, since you didn't get a chance to steal anything."

Burke felt generous at the moment, and it wasn't as if there was any real harm done. He had arrived in time to prevent that from happening, but he would definitely take a little something for himself in compensation.

"What are you talking about?" Confusion filled her eyes. "I was cleaning your cabin and now I'm finished. I accidentally knocked over your case, but everything seems to be all right." She motioned to the paper-filled open case on the floor. "I'll just get my coat and leave."

"Cleaning out the cabin is more like it," Burke answered in a harsh voice. She had that innocent act down pat. If he hadn't caught her red-handed, shuffling through his briefcase, he would probably buy her little performance. Reaching down, he snapped the lid closed and set the case safely on the kitchen table. Never once did his eyes leave her face. "And if you don't want me to go to the police, you should start being a little nicer to me. I already told you I'll take what you're offering in reparation."

He drew her into his arms and captured her mouth with his. She immediately started to struggle.

"Easy, take it easy," he muttered as he banded one arm around her back to keep her in place and placed his other hand on her bottom to pull her tight to his arousal.

"God, you feel good," he groaned. "Open your mouth."

His tongue slipped between her lips as she opened her mouth to speak. He didn't want to talk. He lost himself in the warmth of her mouth and sought her tongue. Rubbing it. Stroking it. She leaned into his kiss, and he pulled back to nibble on her luscious lips. He deepened the kiss again, howling in pain as she clamped her teeth down. Hard.

"Damn it," he cursed as he jerked away from her. The little witch had actually bit him. He barely had time to duck away from her open hand before it made contact with his face.

"How dare you!" Her voice shook with rage as she faced him. Her outraged stance fired up his temper, which had never really had a chance to dissipate.

"Oh, I dare all right. You're the one in trouble, if you haven't forgotten."

"You arrogant, overbearing jerk!" Her voice rose higher with every word until the last one was yelled in his face. With her hands fisted on her hips and her head tossed back, she looked magnificent as she let him have it. "I have a cleaning contract for these cabins and you're a day early checking in. Since no one was here, I decided to go ahead and clean it. Then, all of a sudden, I'm being manhandled and accused of all sorts of things."

Burke began to contemplate the rare fact that, for the second time today, he had made an error in his thinking.

"And furthermore," she continued, "how dare you suggest that *I should be nice to you*, I believe is how you put it, so you won't call the police. I'd rather you did call the police."

Burke's feelings of contrition about the whole incident had completely vanished by the time she'd uttered her last statement. "What did you mean by that last crack? There was a minute there, before you bit me, when you were kissing me as much as I was kissing you."

"That's only because you caught me off guard with your Neanderthal tactics."

His temper evaporated the longer he stared at her and noticed the fine trembling in her body and the trace of fear in her eyes. Ever so gently, Burke drew her into his arms and carefully wrapped his arms around her shaking shoulders. Tentatively, he rubbed his big hand slowly up and down her back, wanting only to comfort her. He may have done a lot of questionable things in his life, but he'd never scared or hurt a woman, until now. He didn't like the feeling.

Burke held her as she continued to tremble in his arms, and he belatedly thought about everything he had said and done since he had walked into the cabin. The small sob that escaped her filled him with shame. "I'm sorry," he whispered softly in her ear. "I'm so very sorry."

Dani stood quietly in the arms of a virtual stranger and let him comfort her. She was held captive by his unexpected gentleness, protected and surrounded by the same strength that had felt so threatening only moments before. It had been a long time since anyone had held her when she needed comfort, and she had almost forgotten how good it felt.

"Hello, anybody here?"

The voice from the living room was like being hit in the face with a bucket of cold water. Turning away from Burke, she angrily swiped at the tears on her face with the back of her hand. She was almost surprised and vaguely disappointed when he let her go. Berating herself for even allowing him to embrace her, she ran her hands over her hair and straightened her sweater. She hoped she looked calm and composed as she grabbed her supply box and held it in front of her like a shield just as Mr. Carter strolled into the kitchen.

"Hello, Mr. Black. I'm Silas Carter. We spoke on the phone earlier today." The older man extended his hand as he spoke. "I brought out that rental agreement for you to sign and to make sure you had everything you needed. I see you've met Dani."

Silas turned to her after he'd shaken Burke's hand. "Any trouble getting this place cleaned today? I know this job was short notice for you."

"No trouble at all, Mr. Carter." Dani thought she managed to answer in an even tone, although her insides were still shaking. The box in her hand moved slightly as her arms trembled. She moved quickly before he noticed anything amiss. "If you'll excuse me, I have to get going."

Leaving the men behind her in the kitchen, Dani rushed to the living room and dropped her supplies on the floor. She jerked her parka on, yanked on her boots, reached down, grabbed her belongings, and bolted out the front door. Her coat was wide open, and the cold hit her immediately. She didn't mind the biting sting of the cold. In fact, she welcomed it. Maybe it would bring her back to her senses. Right now, she needed desperately to get home, where everything felt normal and safe.

Burke's gut clenched as he watched his mystery woman all but run through the front door. The parka she had tugged on looked very familiar.

"You said her name was Dani?" he asked the man standing at his side.

"Yes, Dani O'Rourke. I'm sorry, I thought the two of you would have introduced yourselves."

"No," Burke replied. "We didn't really have time." Burke shook his head, he really had dug himself a deep hole with this particular woman. It would take more than an apology to get on her good side, but first things first. "Let's get that lease signed, and I'll get moved in."

Chapter Three

Dani was still shaking when she turned her truck onto Peach Street. All she wanted was to get home to the little white bungalow at the end of the street. Maybe when she was safe inside, she would stop shaking. Maybe then she could admit that only half of her was afraid. The other half wanted to examine what had happened to her. She had never felt that way before, had never lost control of herself like that.

As she turned the truck into the driveway, she told herself not to take the incident too seriously. After all, she was an adult, and it was only a kiss. The man was a complete stranger, and she would probably never see him again. She should just forget the whole bizarre experience.

Now if only her legs would listen to her, she thought as she climbed out of the driver's seat. She hoped they would hold her up long enough for her to get into the house and curl up at the kitchen table with a nice cup of hot chocolate. By heavens, after the day she had put in, she deserved some chocolate.

Just as she reached back into the truck a long arm shot past hers and snagged the packages sitting on the front seat. Dani jumped, spun around, and knocked one of the packages to the ground.

"Are you all right?"

She looked up into the concerned familiar face staring down at her and sighed. "I'm fine, Patrick. Just a little tired."

"Well, it's no wonder you're tired. Trying to finish Christmas shopping and work too. And I know how much you love to shop." Patrick grinned playfully.

It was a running joke in their family that Dani, the only female, hated to shop, while Patrick and their younger brother, Shamus, both loved it. She'd even been known to try bribery to get out of grocery shopping. Homemade chocolate cake was the bribe of choice.

Patrick leaned down and snatched the package off the ground and then shook it. "Anything in this for me?"

"Anyone would think you were a little boy of nine instead of a grown man of nineteen," she teased.

"You're never too old for presents." Patrick continued to examine the package as he led the way around the house and in through the back door.

Dani followed her brother toward the back door, shaking her head as she went. In spite of her teasing, she was quite proud of the man he was becoming. He had finished high school this past June and had gotten a job with a company that did landscaping all summer and snow-clearing all winter. On top of that, he took night courses in criminology at the local college. He loved his studies and excelled in all his courses. He was seriously considering police work, and while she was proud of him, she worried about this career path.

Stomping her feet on the back step to rid her boots of some of the snow that clung to them, she then stepped in through the back door. There she removed all her winter garb, hanging her coat on the brass hook on the wall and placing her boots on the mat to dry before finally stepping into the snug little kitchen that, to her, signified she was home.

She loved the little kitchen with its pine cupboards and table that shone in the winter sunshine streaming through the window over the kitchen sink. The countertop was the same country blue as the tiles that covered the floor. Kitchen chairs painted to match were positioned around the pine table, two on either side. A planter box on the windowsill overflowed with sage, oregano, and other herbs she used for cooking.

Dani was proud of her kitchen. She and her two brothers had done all the work together and it was the first room they had redone after she had started working. What they hadn't known how to do, they had learned from how-to books from the library. It had made the house seem more like theirs, and not their parents'. It had made them closer as a family.

"Dani, are you sure you're all right? You're awfully quiet."

"I'm fine really. I was just thinking about something that happened at work today." Dani had spoken before her brain registered the fact that this was something she didn't want her brothers to know about. They never kept secrets from each other, but this was just a little too personal.

"What happened? Did anyone give you any problems?" Patrick scowled darkly.

"It's nothing, really. Just a run-in with the new tenant out at the Cabins. He was early checking in and thought that I was breaking and entering, instead of cleaning and mopping." Dani finished with a forced little laugh trying to make light of what had happened.

"Did this guy give you a hard time, Dani? Because if he did, I'm going to go out there and have a little chat with him." Patrick's hands clenched into fists as he spoke.

Dani stared at her brother. Dear heavens, he looked and sounded just like their father. Patrick was still growing but already he was over 6 feet tall and was filling out in the shoulders. Dani didn't doubt that one day he would be built like a large bear of a man, just as their father had been. Right now all that was missing, besides a little more muscle, was the full beard that their father had worn. A lock of hair the color of mahogany fell across his forehead, and the eyes that captured her in their gaze were stormy gray.

"When did you grow up?" she asked in a bewildered tone.

Patrick just glared at her. "Don't change the subject. Did this guy say anything to you?"

Dani sat down at the kitchen table, suddenly very tired. "No." She rubbed her hand across her forehead. "He threatened to call the police at first, but we got it all straightened out."

"He said he was sorry," she added quickly as she saw the anger on Patrick's face when she mentioned the police. All she wanted to do was just forget the whole afternoon.

He stared at her for a long time, as if trying to make up his mind what he should do. Finally, he shook his head and offered her a small grin. "Why don't you go upstairs and take a hot bath?" Resting his hands on her shoulders, he gave them a gentle squeeze. "I'll start supper."

N. J. Walters

"Thanks, you're an angel, Patrick." Pushing herself out of her chair, she gave her brother a quick peck on the cheek before she headed down the hall toward the stairs. She was very relieved to note that his anger seemed to have disappeared as quickly as it had appeared. Thank heavens she had handled that. She hadn't realized that Patrick had grown so protective of her. Well, it was over and done with as far as she was concerned, and she would forget all about Burke Black. She almost believed herself too.

Dani gave her hair a final brush while she studied herself in the mirror. She felt more like herself again now that she'd had a long, hot, bubble-filled soak in the tub and put on her old faded blue sweatpants and sweatshirt. They weren't fit to wear in public as the cuffs were frayed and the knees and elbows were practically white, but she could never bring herself to throw them out. Whenever she was tired or out of sorts, wearing them always made her feel comforted and safe. Kind of a security blanket she wrapped herself in when she knew the rest of the world wasn't watching and judging her.

The smell of oregano and tomato wafted past her as she headed downstairs, and she knew that Patrick had whipped up some of his famous spaghetti sauce. Both her brothers could cook and they all took turns, but no one made spaghetti sauce as tasty as Patrick did. Dani's stomach growled in anticipation, just as the doorbell rang.

"I hope whoever it is, they don't stay," Dani muttered to herself. She was starving and didn't want to wait for supper. She reached the front door, pulled it open, and promptly lost her appetite.

"Miss O'Rourke, I'd really like to speak with you for a minute if I could."

"I don't see that we have anything to say to each other, Mr. Black." Leaning on the door to support her suddenly unsteady legs, she was surprised that her voice sounded so calm when she felt so shaky inside. She'd really never expected to see him again, much less find him on her front doorstep.

"Can I help you with anything?" Dani felt Patrick walk up and stand behind her as he spoke. His solid presence reassured her. Mr. Black was in her home territory now.

"I just wanted to speak to Dani for a moment." He looked as if he might say more, but his lips drew together in an angry line, and he said nothing more as he glared at her brother.

"Are you the guy who threatened my sister today?" Without warning, she found herself staring at the back of her brother's shirt as he pushed his way in front of her.

"Your sister..." Burke trailed off and gave a small chuckle.

"If you find it so funny, maybe we should just step around back and discuss just what happened." Patrick had one foot almost out the door before she even thought to stop him.

"Please, Patrick." Grabbing him by the back of his of his sweatshirt, she held on tight. "Don't do this."

Burke braced his legs apart and faced Patrick. "I really did come to apologize for what happened. For both things. These are for you, Dani." From behind him, he produced a bouquet of long-stemmed red roses and thrust them toward her.

"Maybe she doesn't want your flowers."

Her head started to ache again, the relaxation she'd gotten out of her long hot bath was destroyed, and darn it all, she was hungry. She glared angrily at both of them. "We might as well finish this discussion inside. I'm sure that by now the neighbors have quite enough to talk about."

Dani reached out and plucked the flowers from Burke's hand. Turning her back on both of them, she marched toward the kitchen. They could either follow her or beat each other to a pulp. At this point, she wasn't sure she really cared. She had reached the end of her patience with overbearing men today.

Opening the cupboard door over the kitchen sink, she took down a Mason jar to fill with water. There were no fancy vases in her house, so the roses would just have to make do. She took her time and arranged the roses in the jar and glanced at the door before burying her noses in the buds. The fragrance was almost intoxicating, and the soft petals tickled her nose. Sighing, she carefully carried them to the table and placed them in the center. She'd never had roses before, and they really were beautiful.

The sound of footsteps in the hall made her turn and she cautiously watched Patrick and Burke as they entered the kitchen. There was tension between them, but at least they hadn't come to blows. Dani didn't really know if this should encourage her or not. Before she could decide, the back door opened and Shamus barged in.

"Boy, it's cold out there today. I almost froze onto the gas pumps." Shamus started to pull off his gray Greer's Grocery and Gas Bar coveralls. He worked there part-time, two days a week after school and on Saturdays. "Who owns the truck in the driveway?"

Shamus stopped tugging on the coverall snaps and extended his hand when he saw Burke standing in the kitchen. "Hi, I'm Shamus."

"Burke Black." Burke shook the extended hand. He judged the boy to be about sixteen and definitely Dani's brother. As tall as Dani, he also shared her exact hair and eye color. The biggest difference was in their facial structure. Dani's features were soft and feminine, while Shamus's face was harsh and angular like his older brother. But, unlike his brother, Shamus was smiling.

Shamus seemed to sense the tension in the air as he shook hands with the stranger in their kitchen. "Is anything wrong?"

"No, nothing is wrong," Dani firmly assured her younger brother. "I met Burke today at work and we had a slight misunderstanding, but it's finished now." She punctuated this statement by giving both him and Patrick a pointed look. "Now we're going to set an extra plate on the table, and then we're going to sit down and have a pleasant supper." Dani silently stared at them all, one at a time, as if daring any one of them to disagree with her. Burke just nodded, doing his best to hide his growing good humor.

Shamus finished taking of his boots and coveralls, washed up at the kitchen sink, and then started pulling plates out of the cupboard. Patrick turned his attention to the pots on the stove. Dani was getting down glasses and pouring milk into them.

Burke looked around, slightly bemused, not quite knowing what to do with himself. He sat when Dani directed him to a

35

chair at the end of the table, and in less than five minutes, there was a plate of food in front of him.

He had no idea how he had ended up sitting around a small kitchen table with the O'Rourke family. He was a man used to fine restaurants and intimate dinners for two. As a child, he had been used to grabbing food wherever he could get it. But this, this was something he'd never experienced before.

It was actually fascinating to watch how they interacted with one another. They talked and laughed, asking about each other's day, and seemed to care about the answers. They were always touching each other. Shamus had hugged his sister before he'd sat down to supper. Patrick and Shamus had batted at each other as they fought over a piece of garlic bread. Somehow, he'd found himself in the middle of all this.

"You said you needed to apologize for both things that happened today. What else happened?" Patrick asked, reminding Burke of what he had said earlier.

"Well, it seems as if this whole day was against me from the start." To his surprise, Burke was a little embarrassed to admit he had mistaken Dani for a guy. He recounted the whole story for Patrick and Shamus and was relieved when both brothers laughed. Then he glanced at Dani.

Dani had turned a bright pink as her brothers laughed. "It could have happened to anyone, Patrick, so stop laughing. I was wearing your old parka with the hood zipped right up over my face."

"And you," she turned to Burke, "you didn't have to tell them that you thought I looked like a man."

Way to go, Burke, you sure know how to dazzle a woman. What was it about this woman that made him lose his normal intelligence? For a man who was known for being a smooth operator, he had really lost his touch today.

He spoke quickly to try and salvage the situation. "It really was the coat. There's no other way that I'd take you for anything but a woman." He followed this statement with a long look at Dani. "My mind was on other things, or I never would have made such an obvious mistake."

Shamus, with all the tact of a teenager, asked, "What other things?"

Burke was taken aback by the question. The people he'd associated with minded their own business and expected the same in return. It was strange to have anyone ask about his private life, but since Shamus seemed interested, Burke thought a moment and then answered, "I was actually hoping my leg would hold up."

"Is something wrong with your leg?" Dani asked, concern evident in her voice.

Burke didn't reply immediately. He was bewildered by the fact that she seemed to be genuinely concerned. He couldn't remember a time when anyone had seemed to even remotely care about his health, not when they had nothing to gain from it. He replied before he gave himself time to come to his senses.

"I was in a car accident about five months ago. A guy ran a red light and struck my car going through. He hit on my side and my leg had a bone shattered and there was some muscle and ligament damage as well. It bothers me when I overdo things, but I'm walking and that's all that matters." Burke fell

37

silent as he thought about all he had been through, absently rubbing the scar on the side of his face.

"Oh, Burke, I'm so sorry."

Her soft voice brought Burke back from his thoughts. Her face was pale, and she actually looked as if she was fighting back tears.

"I'm alive. That's all that matters." Burke picked up his fork and started eating, not comfortable having his life discussed by virtual strangers.

"I bet your family is glad you're okay," Shamus said.

"I don't have any family. But that's okay," he added quickly. "I've been on my own forever and that's just the way I like it." He knew he sounded cold and uncaring but he couldn't help himself. The last thing he wanted was pity. He didn't need it from anyone. He shoveled in another bite of supper, wondering if he should just leave.

"So are you here for a holiday, or are you working?" Patrick pumped him for information.

"I sold my business and I guess you can say I'm on medical leave until I decide where I want to go from here. A business associate vacationed up here with his family last year and I remembered how much he said they enjoyed it here. It seemed a likely spot to rethink things. And besides, it's great countryside, and you can't beat the off-season rates."

As far as Burke was concerned, nobody needed to know any more about him or his reasons for being there. Most of the people who knew him through business would never leave the city, and if they did, they stayed in posh exclusive resorts, so there was little to no chance of running into any acquaintances.

The people of Jamesville would know only what he told them about himself and no more.

"I guess it must have been the last straw for you today when you thought I was stealing your stuff." Dani seemed thoughtful as she spoke.

"Well, I was just a little upset. That was all my worldly goods, including my stereo and my computer." Burke teased her, knowing she'd remember how angry he had been. He expected her to come right back with a snappy comment, but she continued to sit quietly.

Patrick pushed back his chair, stood, and grabbed his plate. "Dani, why don't you help Shamus with his English assignment? Burke and I will do the dishes."

Dani stood, but seemed unsure if it was safe to leave the two of them together, so Burke took the choice from her. "You go ahead and help Shamus. I'll dry the dishes. It's the least I can do for such a great meal."

Seemingly reluctant, she finally left the kitchen with Shamus. Burke cleared the table while Patrick started running hot water for the dishes. They worked without speaking for a minute or two before Patrick broke the heavy silence.

"Listen, I'm not sure what really went on today, but I can tell you one thing. If you hurt Dani, you'll be in for a world of hurt all your own." Patrick stopped washing dishes long enough to glare at Burke. "She's special, so unless you're going to treat her right, keep your distance."

Burke finished wiping a plate and carefully placed it in the cupboard before he replied. "Do you always lecture Dani's male friends?" Burke was slightly amused by the fatherly lecture.

"Dani's never really had much in the way of male friends, and she's never asked one to stay for dinner before either." Patrick scrubbed at the pot that had held the spaghetti sauce with more force than was necessary.

Burke stopped drying a glass, staring at Patrick's angry profile. "Why not? Are all the men in this town blind?"

Patrick looked Burke straight in the eye. "No. Most guys don't want to date a woman who has to support two younger brothers."

Patrick turned his attention back to scrubbing the already clean pot. "Dani's given up a lot for us, she's missed out on a lot of things that women do when they're young. She never had a prom night because she dropped out of school to go to work to support us. Then she went back to school at night so she could get her high school diploma. She's always worked hard so Shamus and I could have things. Don't mess with her feelings."

Burke was impressed by her brother's protective attitude toward her, but he was also determined to set his own ground rules. "We just met today. Don't make more of this than it is. Besides, Dani is a grown woman, Patrick. She can do whatever she wants."

"As long as we understand each other. You're welcome here if Dani wants you to be here." Patrick let the dirty water down the drain, wiped the sink clean, and hung the dishcloth to dry.

Just then, the woman under discussion poked her head in the kitchen. "If you guys are finished, can we go out and look for a Christmas tree tonight? I want to get it up in the stand so we can decorate the whole house tomorrow night. Burke, you can come too. If you want to, that is. You might have other plans." Dani came to an abrupt stop, as if aware she was babbling.

"I'd love to go." Burke's smile was wide, and he realized, genuine. "I've never actually picked out a Christmas tree before." It was only after the words were out of his mouth that he realized just how much he had revealed about himself with that simple statement. He cursed himself silently for not having sense enough to keep quiet.

Patrick stared at Burke for a long second and then casually spoke. "There are certain things you need to look for in a good tree…"

They were still discussing them when they all piled into Burke's larger truck and headed to the downtown tree lot.

Chapter Four

The very next evening, Burke stood on the front porch of the little house on Peach Street. Staring at the closed door, he recalled how soft and cuddly Dani had looked standing there yesterday. In an old sweat suit that no woman he'd ever known would be caught dead in, and with her long hair flowing down to her waist, she'd looked more beautiful than any other woman he'd ever seen. And he'd seen his share of gorgeous women. They had always come to him, attracted by his wealth and status. He'd never had to look for a female companion. So why was he freezing his butt off staring at Dani's front door? What was it about this particular woman that made all his masculine instincts stand up and shout *Mine*?

The anger and disappointment he'd felt when he'd seen Patrick for the first time had shocked him. He'd never stopped to think that she might have a boyfriend, or even be married, because she hadn't worn a wedding ring.

Even though Patrick had turned out to be her brother, the feelings Burke was left with made him uncomfortable. But he was determined. He still wanted Dani, no doubt about it, but only on his terms. They were both adults and could enjoy a mature relationship.

For a man used to sophisticated pursuits, such as the theatre and the opera, he was surprisingly excited about tonight. He told himself it was because he liked to see a project through to the end, and after all, he had helped to pick out the tree. He had a responsibility to be there to help decorate it. It wasn't as if being there really meant anything to him. He also knew he was lying to himself. Shaking his head at his unaccustomed feelings, he knocked on the front door.

Shamus flung open the front door and immediately the smell of pine and popcorn filled the air. "Come on in. Dani and I are up to our ears in popcorn. You can help Patrick with the lights."

Shamus turned and strode back to the living room after issuing his orders, leaving Burke to trail behind him. It really was a novelty for anyone to give him orders, but the O'Rourke family seemed to have no trouble doing so. A grin of amusement tugged at his mouth, even as he followed Shamus.

Burke stopped in the archway to the living room, his grin slowly fading as he became enthralled by the picture within. Dani sat on a worn plush green sofa with a big bowl of popcorn in her lap and a needle in her hand. She was absorbed in stringing pieces of the popcorn onto a long thread and hummed along to the Christmas song that played on the stereo. Shamus sprawled at her feet with a bowl of popcorn all his own. Patrick sat on the floor on the other side of the room, surrounded by strings of lights. It was like a scene from a 'Home for Christmas'

Hollywood movie. And although Burke wanted to join them, he suddenly felt as if he was somehow intruding.

As if Dani sensed his hovering presence, she looked at him and smiled a wide, welcoming smile. "Burke, we're glad you could come." Her voice sounded a little breathless.

Lord, she really was a beauty. Even wearing jeans and a blue v-neck sweater, she was breathtaking. Her eyes glowed with happiness and her lips were parted slightly as she smiled at him. All he could think about was tasting those soft luscious lips. He could feel his body reacting to the very sight of her and was helpless to stop it. He had always had ruthless control over his desires, deciding when he would fulfill his bodily needs and with whom. But this shy woman made a mockery of his control. He didn't like it, but he figured he'd regain his control once they slept together and the novelty wore off. Then he would be back in control of the situation.

"Every year we pack these things away properly and every year they come out in a tangle." Patrick held up a clump of lights in one hand. "You can give me a hand with these if you'd rather not string popcorn. I need all the help I can get."

"I'll see what I can do." Burke settled himself on the floor next to Patrick. He glanced up and saw that Dani was still smiling at him.

"Now that everyone's here, I'll get the eggnog and potato chips." Setting her bowl aside, Dani stood and headed toward the kitchen.

She really had to get a hold of herself. Just because a good-looking man was in her living room was no reason to make a fool of herself. Burke wore a pair of faded jeans and a simple cream-colored fisherman's knit sweater. But the way he filled out his clothes should be considered lethal and dangerous to a woman's peace of mind. He made her stomach all fluttery, and Dani felt more like a teenager than a grown woman. If she weren't careful, she'd find herself giggling and that just wouldn't do. She pulled herself together, grabbed her tray of treats, and went back to the living room.

"Food. Great, I'm starving," Shamus announced as Dani placed the tray on the coffee table.

Everyone grabbed a drink and settled back to work. Nobody felt the need to talk, but the room was filled with the soft strains of Christmas music. The smell of cinnamon and popcorn permeated the air, and the quiet was punctuated by the occasional sound of crunching chips.

The men started the dreaded task of putting on the Christmas tree lights as Dani finished stringing the last of the popcorn. "You missed a spot over there," she directed from the sofa.

"But Dani, you said it was fine there five minutes ago." Patrick sighed impatiently, even as he maneuvered a strand of lights to the spot she had pointed out.

"Well now it needs more lights. Don't you think so, Burke?"

"If you think it needs more lights, then I guess it needs more lights," Burke answered diplomatically.

"Smart move, Burke, real slick," Patrick observed. "Now hand me that last set."

Dani just smiled as she watched them work. It seemed so right for Burke to be here with them, working to decorate the

Christmas tree that they had all picked out together. She felt happy inside and somehow knew that Burke was a large part of that happiness. Dani worried about that fact. Burke was still very much a stranger to her. But right now, with all of them here together in the glow of the tree lights, it was hard to be concerned.

When the lights were finished, she began to drape the strings of popcorn on the tree.

"You need more over there," Patrick pointed out from his seat in the rocking chair in the corner.

"I think you just want to get back at me for the lights. It's not my fault that I'm a popcorn-stringing expert." Dani smiled at Patrick as she teased him, but she adjusted the string of popcorn over the branches he had pointed out.

Shamus sized up all sides of the tree. "That's perfect. Now for the ornaments; Dani and our mom made most of them, you know," Shamus stated with obvious pride.

"They're beautiful." Burke examined some of the ornaments laid out on the coffee table. He seemed enthralled by the miniature angels made of lace, happy Santa faces made of bright colored felt, candy canes made of beads, and the multitude of other brightly crafted ornaments. They looked even more delicate as he cradled them in his large hands.

"Well, I try to add one or two new ones every year," Dani added, flushing with a mixture of embarrassment and pleasure at Burke's reaction and his care with her Christmas treasures.

Half an hour later, they hung the last of the ornaments on the tree. The time had passed quickly and was filled with good-natured directions and advice, most of which was ignored. Dani,

Patrick, and Shamus each had favorite ornaments that they placed on the tree, but they encouraged Burke to choose some for himself.

"Now it's time for the tree topper." Patrick passed a delicate porcelain blonde angel to Dani.

"I think Burke should have the honor this year." She handed him the angel as she spoke.

He stared at the fragile lace angel lying in his large hands. "I really shouldn't. It's your job."

He protested lightly, but Dani could tell that a part of him wanted to do it. "We want you to." Dani encouraged him further by gently tugging him to the stepladder.

As they stood and watched, Burke stepped up onto the ladder and placed the angle at the top of the tree.

The men packed away the empty boxes in the storage closet under the stairs while Dani gave the floor a quick vacuum. Then they all retired to the living room to view their masterpiece and debate who had done the best job of them all. Burke's leg was tired, but overall he felt good. He felt even better an hour later when Patrick and Shamus, who both had to work in the morning, went up to bed.

Sighing with contentment, Burke sat on a worn sofa with his feet propped up on a scarred pine coffee table and a glass of eggnog in his hand, feeling more relaxed than he had in months. Dani looked so pretty in the glow from the colored lights. He wasn't sure if she was real or just a figment of his imagination. Actually, he wasn't sure if any of this was real. They all seemed to care so much for one another. It was obvious in the way they acted, but it didn't seem to be an act, it seemed real.

Dani sat by his side on the sofa. Only the lights of the tree lit the room and the stereo played carols softly in the background. Despite the angel peering down at them from above, Burke decided that the real angel was sitting on the sofa next to him.

"I'm really glad you came, Burke." She snuggled closer to him, and he tightened his arm around her shoulders. Even knowing Patrick and Shamus were just upstairs, it was all too easy to imagine that they were alone.

"I'm glad, too." Burke inhaled deeply and found himself aroused by the smell of her. She smelled of vanilla and pine, and an elusive scent that was distinctly Dani. He had to have her soon or at least a taste of her. With that thought in mind, he laid his mug on the table beside him.

Cupping her chin in his hand, he gently tilted her face toward his and leaned down to brush his lips across her forehead. Dani leaned into the gentle caress. Her eyes closed as his lips skimmed them ever so softly. Her lips parted on a sigh.

"Please," she whispered. "Please kiss me, Burke."

"Yes," he murmured as he lowered his mouth until it touched hers.

Back and forth, he moved his lips across hers. His tongue reached out to taste her sweetness, and Dani welcomed him.

Burke couldn't help himself. The invitation was too much. His tongue thrust into her mouth, tasting and teasing her. Then he felt her tongue slide tentatively against his, lightly touching and stroking. His control broke.

Turning his body, he eased her back onto the sofa. His arms came around her, and his mouth was hard on hers as his tongue thrust in and out of her mouth in an intoxicating rhythm. He cradled her body close to his, loving the feel of her softness against his hardness.

Unable to stop himself, his large hand stroked up her side and covered her breast through her sweater. She fit perfectly into his hand, and he savored in the feeling as she arched her back, trying to get closer to him.

"You feel so good, so damned good," he muttered as he abandoned her mouth and ran his lips down the side of her neck. She gave herself so readily to him, holding back nothing. Burke knew she wanted him as badly as he wanted her.

His hand left her breast, and Dani cried out with the loss. He hushed her as his hand moved under her sweater, pushed aside her bra, and cupped her bare breast. She shuddered at his touch.

Burke groaned, feeling the slight quivering of her body as he moved his lips back up to devour hers. His hand covered her breast, cupping it and weighing its fullness. Never had he felt skin as soft as hers. He knew he had to see her. Had to taste her.

Pushing her sweater aside, he leaned down and laved her nipple with his tongue. Dani moaned aloud, and he reveled in the sound, rewarding her by taking her nipple into his mouth and suckling gently on her breast.

Never had he tasted anything as good as the woman lying beneath him. It was as if she had been fashioned specifically for him and him alone. When she cried out and arched her hips against him, he thought he might explode. All he wanted was to have her naked skin next to his. He needed to be inside her, watching her shudder and come apart for him.

A thump from upstairs brought with it a cold dose of reality. Even though it almost killed him, he drew his lips from her breast, adjusted her bra, and pulled her sweater back down to cover her upper body. She didn't seem to understand why he was drawing away and tried to pull him back to her.

"No Dani, we have to stop." He knew he sounded harsh, but damn it he was hurting. She had to know he was hurting.

"What's wrong?" she questioned in a small, bewildered voice.

Burke felt her stiffen in his arms and start to pull away. He didn't like the feeling, so he stopped her by simply wrapping his arms around her. "This isn't the time or place for this, Dani. Your brothers are just upstairs."

"I can't believe I forgot them." She gave a nervous laugh as she sat up. This time when she gently pulled away, he let her go.

"You're right. That got out of hand." She watched him as if gauging his reaction. "It should never have gone that far."

Burke gave her a little hug and released her. "I can wait for a better time."

Burke couldn't wait to get Dani alone so he could finally have her. It never occurred to him that she would deny him. After all, he had never been denied in his whole adult life. He knew he would have her, so for now he was content to plan her seduction.

Dani watched the lights of Burke's truck disappear into the night. She hugged herself in the darkness, still unsettled by what had happened. Her body still ached, wanting something it had never had before. She'd never been with a man, and when he'd pulled away from her so suddenly, she'd been afraid that she'd disappointed him with her inexperience.

Part of her wanted him to continue, but she was glad that he stopped. All the feeling and emotions that had flooded her system had left her shaken. She knew she was drawn to Burke, but she wanted time to get to know him better. In her heart, she knew she couldn't give herself to him until she was sure of her feelings for him and his for her. She was in no hurry. There was plenty of time to explore this relationship.

Unplugging the tree lights, she left the dark living room behind and climbed the stairs. Going through her nightly ritual, she readied herself for bed. She was still reliving the wonder of their kisses when she finally drifted off to sleep.

Chapter Five

"Merry Christmas! And what a wonderful day it is. The sun is shining and there's a fresh layer of snow on the ground. Not so great for mom and dad, but great for all those new sleds you kids got for Christmas."

Burke ignored the perky female voice, flicked off the radio alarm, and looked at the clock. It was only 7:00 A.M., but he had been invited to Christmas breakfast at the O'Rourke home and had been promised blueberry pancakes. He felt a strange anticipation as he climbed out of bed and headed for the shower. Today was the day.

The floor was cold beneath his feet, but he didn't stop to turn up the heat. He would be gone all day and hopefully all night. The bathroom was as barren as the rest of the cabin. A toothbrush and toothpaste were tucked away inside the medicine chest along with his razor and aftershave. The only signs of habitation were the bar of soap on the side of the shower stall and the towel and facecloth hanging on the towel rack.

As he adjusted the water temperature and stepped under the spray, his body started to tense as he thought about the coming night. He knew that Patrick and Shamus would spend Christmas Day at home, but this evening they were going to make the rounds to their friends' homes. He and Dani would be alone then.

His body became slightly aroused in anticipation. But then, it seemed that he had been in a constant state of partial arousal ever since he had met Dani. The more he thought about that fact, the more he didn't like it. He had never allowed a woman to have this much control over him. She was always in his thoughts, especially since the night they had put up the Christmas tree.

He had picked out her Christmas present with care. He knew that Dani thought he didn't have much money, and he hadn't corrected her assumption. He couldn't just buy her expensive jewelry like he usually did for whatever woman he happened to be seeing when the holidays rolled around. Christmas wasn't a big deal to him, but he had learned that women seemed to think a lot of it. The earrings he had picked out were simple thick gold hoops. Not much money by his standards, but he thought they would suit Dani, classy without being showy. He figured Christmas Day and her present would put her in a good mood. Women always appreciated jewelry.

He believed that if he finally had her in his bed for a whole night, he would be able to work her out of his system. Yes, once he'd learned all her secrets he could put her to the back of his mind and start concentrating on more important things. Like what in the hell he was going to do with the rest of his life. But, there was no reason they couldn't enjoy a healthy relationship while he was contemplating his options. It would clear his mind and help him think better.

Feeling confident about things, he stepped out of the shower and toweled off. He shaved quickly, hung the towel to dry, and went back to the bedroom to dress. He stopped in the kitchen long enough to snag his jacket and keys and he was out through the front door. Right now he had a breakfast date to get to.

"Deck the halls with boughs of holly." Dani sang along to the music on the stereo as she danced around the kitchen, stirring batter for blueberry pancakes. This was the most wonderful Christmas she'd had in years, and she knew that Burke was the reason why. Oh, she always loved this time of year. The hustle and bustle, getting together with friends, secrets, cookies, just everything. But this year was unusual because she finally had someone special to share it with.

She felt as if Burke really understood her. Since the night they had decorated the Christmas tree, he had not pushed the physical side of their relationship. There had been cuddles and good night kisses that made her toes curl just thinking about them, but he hadn't pushed her any further. Things really had been moving much too fast for her. She could barely look at the sofa without blushing.

She had certainly enjoyed what had happened. Every time she thought about it, she got all warm and achy inside. Burke could very well be the man for her, but she needed time to get to know him better. Dani knew she had to be sure she loved him and that he loved her before she could give herself to him.

Maybe she was being unrealistic, but she wanted a relationship as loving as her parents' had been. Her parents had had their ups and downs and the occasional fight, but there had never been any doubt that they had loved one another. Settling for less was not an option.

But things were going so well. She knew she was already half in love with him. She thought about him constantly and found herself wanting to share her thoughts and life with him. Burke had spent every evening of this last week at the house with her and the boys. Just sharing meals, helping Shamus with a business assignment for school that was due after the holidays, watching television; little things that had helped her to learn more about him as a man.

For one thing, he seemed to know a lot about business. Dani would never ask him outright, but she was sure he'd had to sell his business because of the accident, maybe to pay hospital debts or maybe because he wasn't physically able to handle the routine anymore. She was certain he would tell her what had happened, when he was ready. She wouldn't ask though, because she knew all about male pride. It was easily wounded and hard to heal. That's what her mother had always said, and it had always guided her actions with Patrick and Shamus. She would trust it to work with Burke. It was better to wait for him to bring it up.

She was confident that when Burke decided on his next business venture, he would make a success of it. In her heart, she knew she wanted to be the woman who worked next to him to make it so. She was no stranger to hard work, and it really wouldn't be work if it meant they were building a life together.

She could picture it in her mind. She would run her business and help Burke with his business venture. Maybe they would buy an old farmhouse, have two or three children, and get a dog. Children definitely needed a dog. It would be perfect.

"Earth to Dani." Patrick's deep voice startled her, and she jumped, barely catching the bowl before it slipped from her grasp.

She laughed as she realized that she'd been standing in the middle of the kitchen, a spoon held upright in one hand, staring into space. "You caught me wool-gathering. Merry Christmas, Patrick." She placed the bowl safely on the counter before she turned and wrapped her arms around her brother, hugging him tight.

Patrick smiled as he hugged her back. "What were you doing, counting all the loot you got for Christmas?"

"You're the one who does that, not me. I'm busy getting things ready for breakfast, so as soon as Burke gets here, we can go straight to the presents."

"So you were thinking about presents?"

"Maybe," Dani answered thoughtfully, flushing a little.

Shamus bound into the kitchen like an exuberant puppy, practically quivering with excitement. "Can we open the presents now?"

"As soon as Burke gets here. Here, have some hot chocolate." She handed him a mug steaming with chocolate.

"I'll go watch from the window. Did you tell him early?" Shamus asked as he left the room without waiting for an answer.

"Yes, I told him early. Your presents aren't going anywhere without you."

"You know what kids are like, Dani." Patrick assumed a serious adult look on his face. "I think I'll go watch with him."

Her laughter trailed after him as he left the kitchen. They were all little boys at heart. She told herself it was just for their sake that she poured a cup of chocolate for herself and went to the window to watch with them.

Sitting amidst a pile of discarded wrapping paper, Burke suddenly felt as if he understood the story of *Alice in Wonderland*. You enjoyed yourself in the strange new land, but you were always alert, never sure just what the inhabitants were going to do next. Every moment was an adventure.

This was a far cry from his usual Christmas morning. More often than not, he unwrapped any presents he had received from clients and staff on Christmas Eve. Christmas morning, he slept late, rising just in time to dress and go eat a quiet lunch at an elegant restaurant. If he was seeing anyone at the time, he escorted her to dinner. Dinner was usually followed by a trip to her apartment where she showed him how much she liked whatever expensive bauble he had bought her. Year to year, the only thing that varied was the woman, but even that, he controlled. It was just another decision in an endless line of executive decisions.

This morning had been quite chaotic. He had been met at the door with several commands to hurry. Then he'd been hustled into the living room where chaos had reigned. Paper had been ripped from packages, and presents had been oohed and aahed over. Laughter had filled the room as they had eaten chocolate Santa's and examined their presents more closely once the immediate flurry had ended.

Burke had been surprised to find that there were presents under the tree for him as well. He had opened the first small package to find a pewter keychain with a Christmas tree dangling from the end of it from Patrick.

"Just so you remember your Christmas with us," Patrick said gruffly. "No big deal."

But it was a big deal to Burke, a very big deal. Shamus had gifted him with a red and white striped scarf, eerily reminiscent of the Cat in the Hat. Dani had shyly handed him a larger package.

"I hope you like it. If it doesn't fit or you don't like it, we can always exchange it." Dani looked uncertain about her present. Her hands were nervously shredding wrapping paper as she waited for him to unwrap his present.

Burke held the sweater in front of him, slightly stunned by the extravagance of it. He knew that Dani didn't have a lot of extra money and this sweater had to have cost her. It was a hand-knit bulky pullover sweater with a cozy cabin scene on the front. In fact, it looked a lot like the cabin he was staying in. He looked at her expectant face. "It's beautiful." And he sincerely meant it.

"I thought it would remind you of where we met. I couldn't find one with two people pushing a car out of a snowbank." Dani shared a smile and a look with him. Neither one of them was likely to forget their first two meetings.

"This is the best present anyone has ever given me. But you shouldn't have spent so much." Burke knew he had received more expensive gifts in the past, but never one more personal.

"It wasn't really that expensive," she answered, even though it obviously was. "I clean house for an older woman who knits them for the boutique in town." Burke stared at the sweater, wondering how many free hours of cleaning Dani would be giving the woman to pay for his present.

"My presents don't seem like much after these." Burke was suddenly self-conscious; he didn't like the feeling. "Here." He brusquely thrust envelopes at Patrick and Shamus. "I didn't know what you might want, but I remember that when I was your age I never had enough pocket money."

Patrick and Shamus cautiously open their envelopes.

"Hey, this is cool," Shamus exclaimed.

"What is it?" Dani asked, her curiosity apparent.

"Gift certificates." Patrick held his up in the air. "One for the music store, one for the jeans shop, and two movie passes."

"Thanks a lot, Burke. Now I can get that new CD I wanted. What did you get, Dani?"

"Shamus, where are your manners?" Dani scolded. Her cheeks were pink with what appeared to be embarrassment. "You'll have Burke thinking we're a greedy bunch when the presents aren't important. What's really important is that Burke is here with us today. That's present enough."

"Then I guess I'll just have to return this gift to Santa since you don't want it." Burke held a little foil-wrapped package in his hand.

Dani looked instantly contrite. "I didn't say I didn't want it." Her pitiful plea for sympathy was ruined by the mischief in her eyes.

"Well, I guess you can have it. But only if I get those promised pancakes."

"You'll get them as soon as I open my present," she smiled angelically.

"Merry Christmas, Dani." Burke handed her the little box and found he was holding his breath while he waited for her to open it.

"Oh my," Dani exclaimed softly as she opened the little blue velvet box. Tears filled her eyes. "They're beautiful Burke, I've never owned anything so lovely." Her fingers gently caressed the gold hoops nestled on the blue velvet lining.

"Let's see, Dani." Patrick peered over Dani's shoulder for a closer look. "Hey, they're really nice." He slanted a curious look at Burke.

"Dani deserves nice things." Burke got to his feet and began to pick up discarded wrapping paper. "Now where are my pancakes?" He ignored the feeling he got in the pit of his stomach when Dani took the earrings from the box, slipped them in her ears, and went immediately to the mirror in the front hall to admire them.

It was just hunger pains, he told himself, nothing more. It was time for him to take control of the situation. After all, he was not a member of this family, and he probably wouldn't be around for too much longer. He had plans of his own. But his plans suddenly didn't seem very important to him at the moment.

The rest of the day was something Burke knew he would never forget. Dani's homemade blueberry pancakes had melted in his mouth. It had been more of a race between him, Patrick, and Shamus to see who could eat the most. It finished with all of them groaning as they pushed away from the kitchen table with Dani's admonishment of "save room for supper" ringing in their ears.

As soon as breakfast was finished, Burke pulled on his new sweater, wound his scarf around his neck, and left the house with Dani. He walked as close to her as he could get, considering he was loaded down with packages, boxes and bags. Dani knocked on doors all over the neighborhood, distributing presents everywhere she stopped. People were friendly as they chatted with Dani, but more than one person glanced at him with a sly eye.

Burke knew that they were speculating on his relationship with Dani, but no one came right out and asked. In spite of the questions in everyone's eyes, he found himself enjoying the day. Everywhere they went, they were greeted warmly and invited in for coffee and cookies. Burke soon realized that this was a yearly tradition, and everyone had been waiting for Dani's visit.

Mrs. Whitman, an elderly widow who lived across the street from Dani, opened her box as soon as Dani set it in her hands. "Oh my, thank you Dani, I do so look forward to your cherry cake every year. You make it just like your mother did; God rest her soul." She made sure that they had a sampling of her homemade fudge before they left.

Burke helped Dani deliver four more cakes, several boxes of cookies, and gift bags filled with homemade jams before they

61

made their way back to her house. "You realize I'm going to burst when I eat supper."

"You shouldn't have eaten so many cookies then. I swear, Burke, you sampled one of everything."

"I was only trying to be polite," he countered, rubbing his stomach in appreciation. "Besides, I've never seen so many home-baked cookies before. I didn't think people still did that."

"Don't worry," she laughed. "There's still hours until supper. I'm sure you'll be starved by then. You'll find room for turkey. Come on, I'll race you back." Without warning, Dani took off running toward the house and was just bursting through the back door when Burke finally caught up to her.

"I beat you, I beat you," Dani taunted. She did a victory dance around the kitchen, swinging her hips from side to side.

"You had a head start." Burke rubbed his leg that was now throbbing. He was suddenly angry; with himself for caring, at his leg for not working, and at Dani for running.

Dani looked at Burke's taut face and the hand on his leg and all her laughter fled. "I'm sorry," she said quietly. "I shouldn't have run."

She placed her hand on his arm, as if trying to soothe him. "I don't want your damn pity," Burke snapped, unable to stop himself. He pulled his arm away from her touch. "Maybe I should go." He suddenly felt old and tired and jaded.

"No, please stay. We'll curl up on the sofa and watch *A Christmas Carol* on television. After that, it'll be time for supper. I'll feed you more cookies later if you stay."

Burke knew she was trying to cajole him out of his temper and damned if it wasn't working. "All right," he answered, trying to recapture his light-hearted mood. "But only if you make hot chocolate."

"It's a deal."

She held out her hand to him, and he was powerless to do anything but take it.

"This time I mean it. I will burst if I try to eat another morsel of food." Burke groaned as he settled himself onto the sofa next to Dani.

The house was quiet now. The day was winding down. Christmas dinner had been eaten with a great deal of lip-smacking, finger-licking, and plate-scraping. The leftovers had been stored for tomorrow's lunch, and the dishes had been washed, dried, and put away.

Shamus and Patrick had taken off to spend the evening with their friends. It was just the two of them, sitting in the dark with the lights of the Christmas tree shining down on them. It felt right somehow, Dani thought as she moved closer to snuggle into Burke.

"I really enjoyed today. Having you here made it special." She smiled at him even as her fingers toyed with the gold hoops that hung from her ears. "Thank you again for these. They're finer than any I've ever owned."

She realized suddenly that she was happy. Sometime during the day they had spent together, she had realized that Burke was the right man for her. She could no longer lie to herself. She was in love with him. She wasn't quite sure when she had finally admitted it to herself. Maybe it had been when he had seemed so touched by their presents. Maybe it was the way he had happily delivered presents with her, making her feel that there was nowhere else he would rather be. Maybe it was the way he had made her feel today, that she was special. All she knew was that she loved him.

Reaching out, Burke tipped her face upward and turned it so her lips met his. He slowly moved his lips back and forth over hers. Back and forth. Back and forth. Parting her lips on a sigh, her tongue tentatively touched his lips. She didn't know who was seducing whom. That was her last coherent thought.

Dani felt absolutely wonderful. Her insides melted and her heart felt as if it was swelled inside her chest. She knew she loved Burke. She was sure that even if he didn't love her yet, he must have deep feelings for her. The way he kissed her made her feel cared for and cherished. She knew they couldn't go too far, but she wanted to experience some of the wondrous things he had made her feel before. She parted her lips further and tentatively stroked his tongue with hers. Burke groaned and deepened the kiss, and she was lost.

"I want you, Dani. I have to have you."

His arms banded around her, pulling her tight to him. He fell back on the sofa and turned so she was facing him, her back against the sofa and her front tight against his. She could feel the muscles tense in his arms as she ran her hands over his back, urging him closer to her.

When he kissed her again and again, she reveled in it. She arched into his touch as his hand skimmed down over her arm and then across her breast. They ached so much that she rubbed them against his chest, seeking his touch.

He answered her plea, by cupping her breast through her sweater and rubbing his thumb over the taut nipple that was visible through the material. She moaned and pulled his head down so she could kiss him again. She was filled with a yearning so deep that she didn't know what to do. So she hung on tightly to Burke.

Kissing a path from her mouth to her ear, he whispered to her, "Yes, sweetheart, hold me tight. I'll take care of you."

Dani felt Burke's hand as he pushed his way under her sweater. His large hand smoothed over her stomach before moving up to cover the lace of her bra. His fingers traced the lace pattern covering her breasts, and she surrendered herself to the delicious feeling.

"You're so beautifully responsive, Dani." His fingers slipped beneath her bra and caressed her bare breast. His body suddenly went still.

"We're on the sofa in the living room," he muttered. "Come on, sweetheart, let's go up to your room, to bed." He punctuated his statement with kisses.

"To bed?" She was confused. One minute, Burke was kissing her, well, more than kissing her. Now, he had a hard, almost angry look on his face.

She suddenly became aware of just how exposed she was. Her face heated as she felt herself blush. Wrapping her arms around herself, she inadvertently trapped Burke's hand against her aching breast. The pleasure was so great; it was making it almost impossible for her to think straight. "Why would we go to bed?" she asked, her mind still muddled with desire.

"I don't want the boys to walk in on us." His tight smile didn't quite reach his eyes. "I want you spread out on your bed, naked and hot for me." Cupping her breast with his fingers, he gave it a final squeeze before tugging his hand out from between them. "Come on, honey. Let's go."

He reached down to pull her to her feet at the same moment that she pulled back from him.

"Burke," she began nervously. "I didn't mean for things to go this far. I honestly thought you understood that I need time. This is all happening so fast." Dani felt ashamed that she had let things progress to this extent. "I'm sorry."

Burke looked stunned for a moment, and then his eyes darkened with anger. "What exactly do you mean?" The cold, hard tone of his voice made her shiver. It reminded her too much of their first meeting out at the cabin.

The way that she covered herself and the shame in her eyes only seemed to make him even angrier. She desperately searched for a way to make him understand. "I can't sleep with you, Burke. It's too soon. I need time." She brushed her hair out of her face and took a deep breath. "We barely know each other. We're not engaged or even officially dating, for that matter."

His voice was so icy when he finally spoke, she felt as if her skin was being flayed by his words. "I don't mind giving you expensive presents, but don't think you can hold out for marriage. No toss in the sack is worth that."

Looking up into the harsh face that she'd come to love, she searched for some scrap of caring. She barely recognized him. His face was a hard, austere mask and his eyes had never seemed so dark or remote.

As his words registered, she felt such a pain deep inside she thought she would surely die of it. Telling herself she must have misunderstood, she spoke quickly.

"I don't understand what you mean. I know I let things go a little too far. But I thought you understood that I need to go slow, need time to get to know you better." Dani didn't know how something that had started out so beautifully could end up so horribly wrong.

"Come off it, sweetheart." This time the endearment was nothing more than a sarcastic cut. "Don't play innocent with me. You've been encouraging me all week long. I might sleep with you, but I wouldn't marry you, or any other woman." He tugged at the gold hoop in her ear. "I don't mind being good to you, but I'll pay for my pleasure in cash only. Don't expect anything more."

"But I love you," Dani blurted out before she could stop herself. The pain that racked her body was almost too much to bear. She felt the wetness on her face, and somewhere in the back of her mind, she realized she was crying.

"There is no such thing. Only short-term lust." Burke shook all over. His hands clenched at his sides as his anger rolled off him in waves.

"Burke, please understand." She held out her hand, desperate to reach him. She had to stop him before he destroyed something that was incredibly precious.

"I understand all right. If you want to hold out for the highest bidder, go right ahead. There are plenty of other women out there who want what I'll offer." Grabbing his jacket off the back of the chair, he stalked to the door. Pausing when he reached it, he swung around suddenly to face her. "A few words of advice. Don't offer what you're not prepared to deliver. The next fool you entice might just take it anyway." With that parting shot, he walked out of the room.

Dani flinched when the front door slammed. How had this happened? She heard a sound. Almost like an animal in pain, the harsh sound hurt her ears so much that she slapped her hands over her ears. She couldn't shut it out. It wouldn't go away. In some detached part of herself, she was amazed to realize that the sound came from her.

She had to get away from this room. There was no way she could allow her brothers to find her like this. Dragging herself from the room, she somehow managed to climb the stairs to her bedroom and close the door tight behind her. Stumbling across the room, she made it to the bed before she crumbled. Sobs broke from her throat in great gasps, and the tears flowed freely from her eyes.

She had no idea how much time had passed or when she had stopped crying. Her eyes were almost swollen shut, and she could barely swallow because her throat hurt so much. Moving like an old woman, Dani peeled off her clothes, yanked on her flannel nightgown, and crawled into bed. She tunneled under the blankets as if they could somehow protect her from what had happened.

The worst pain of all was in her heart. Simply because there was no pain. She couldn't feel her heart anymore. That was probably a good thing, she reasoned. If her heart was broken, then it wouldn't hurt anymore. She didn't think she could survive any more pain.

She lay awake until the sun started to come up, just staring at the ceiling, not thinking or feeling anything. She had heard both Shamus and Patrick when they had come home, but she hadn't moved. Finally when she could lie there no longer, she dragged herself out of bed and into the shower. She was satisfied that she was numb all over. That was the only way she could survive right now. There was no other way.

Chapter Six

Burke was frustrated and angry. At himself. At Dani. Sitting on the edge of his bed, he scrubbed his hand over his face. Everything was such a mess. Maybe he shouldn't have rushed her. She wasn't like the sophisticated women he normally associated with. Dani had lived a sheltered life, and she had an air of innocence about her that both attracted and repelled him at the same time. Unlike the women who usually shared his bed, Dani had expectations.

As he stared out the window at the winter wonderland, he knew he had no one to blame but himself. He had pushed too quickly. His normally ironclad control over his body was a joke when he was around Dani. He'd been relaxed and almost drunk with pleasure after the best Christmas day he'd ever spent. When she had gone into his arms with such sweet abandon, he'd lost all control. When she'd told him to stop, he'd done something he rarely ever did. He lost his temper.

The depth of his anger had surprised even him. He wanted her more than he had ever wanted any woman before, and she had pushed him away. Then he'd compounded the whole fiasco by letting his anger have a voice. Even those women who were attracted to his money wanted the trappings of romance.

He rose from the bed and padded to the shower. But it wasn't entirely his fault. She had certainly taken her sweet time before she pushed him away. Tempting him with her sweetness. She was a big girl, and she knew the score. He was right to be honest with her about his intentions, but if he hadn't lost his temper he might have been able to work things out with her, given time.

Sleep had eluded him last night. His mind kept replaying the scene over and over until he thought he might just lose his mind. Dani's face, so hurt and vulnerable, had filled his dreams last night. It taunted him while he showered and while he dressed. And it still mocked him as climbed aboard his truck and drove into Jamesville for breakfast.

Burke also had to admit that he didn't like the feelings of rejection he was experiencing. He'd never allowed anyone to get close enough to him to really matter. Therefore, he'd never had to worry about being hurt by anything they might say or do. Somehow, Dani had gotten past his hard earned defenses. He knew he had upset and disappointed her. And that left him feeling out of sorts and inadequate. Not feelings he particularly enjoyed.

But she was hard on a man's ego. He had offered her everything he could give, and she hadn't even considered accepting it. Well, he hadn't been lying when he said there were plenty of other women who would be happy to have him around and give him whatever he wanted. The problem was he didn't want another woman. He only wanted Dani.

Gazing up the main street from behind the wheel of his pickup truck, he realized that the street seemed almost deserted, even though it was past seven o'clock in the morning. Well, he consoled himself; he'd wanted to get away from everything and everyone that he knew. Jamesville was a small town of about five thousand people, not large by major city standards, but large enough to have a thriving business district and an air of prosperity about it.

Main Street, appropriately enough, ran through the center of town and was the focal point for most of the major businesses. The Jamesville Town Hall was an old brick building, that come summer would be almost lost in a sea of green ivy. It had the feel of solidity about it, as if it had stood for a hundred years and would gladly stand for a hundred more. The bank and the police station were also housed in two-story brick buildings, and their close proximity probably discouraged would-be robbers. Although, he imagined they didn't worry too much about that kind of thing here.

The town Christmas tree, complete with lights and decorations, stood in front of city hall, and Burke could only marvel at the fact that all the lights were still there and hadn't been smashed out or ripped off. As he drove toward the end of the street, he passed several stores with festive window displays, but darkened windows. He began to wonder if anyone would even open for business the day after Christmas day. He pulled the truck into an empty parking spot in front of Jessie's Diner and was rewarded with the glow of the lights from within and the open sign that hung on the door.

This town was his home for the next few months. With his obsession with Dani, he'd almost forgot why he'd come here in the first place. A change of lifestyle, a change of pace. Part of that change was learning to slow down and not be so driven. Oh, he was honest enough to acknowledge that he would always be more driven that the average person, but he needed to turn it down a notch. Take the time to enjoy the things that he hadn't before.

Right now, he wanted a cup of coffee and a good breakfast. He knew he still wanted Dani, but on his terms not hers. He'd give them both a few days to cool off and then he'd approach her again, but he wouldn't make the same mistake again. This time he'd go slowly and make sure she understood exactly where he stood on the terms of their relationship.

Feeling better by just having made a decision, he was climbing out of the truck when he heard his name being called. His heart sped up, and he turned quickly, hoping it was Dani. Maybe she had changed her mind about them.

But the figure walking toward him was not the woman he was hoping to see, but the blonde he'd helped getting her car out of the snow. What was her name? Cynthia. That was it. Cynthia James.

"Good morning, Burke. I haven't seen much of you around town." She punctuated this statement by running a red tipped fingernail up and down his left arm.

"Good morning, Cynthia," Burke replied, wondering cynically how much of him she really wanted to see. He knew that his look was hard, and as far as Cynthia knew, he had no money. What was the appeal? What did she want from him?

73

"You don't seem to be getting out much since you came to town. Are you attending the New Year's Eve bash at the Country Club?"

"I really haven't given it much thought, actually."

"You really should consider going. Anyone who's anyone attends." She moved closer to him, practically rubbing against his side.

"I assume you'll be going then." Burke stepped back from her, wondering how far she'd go to fandangle an invitation from him.

"Of course I'll be there." Cynthia gave a little laugh. "It just wouldn't be a New Year's Eve bash without a James there. And since Daddy will be out of town on business, it's up to me to hold up the family honor."

"I'm sure you'll do an admirable job, Miss James."

"Mr. Black." Smiling coyly, she sidled up closer to him again. This time there was no mistaking the brush of her breast across his arm. "Since you're new in town, I consider it my civic duty and indeed my honor to ask you to escort me to this event. You'll get a chance to meet all the important people in town. And maybe we'll find some entertainment you'll enjoy." Her pink tongue came out to lick her lips hungrily as she stared up at him.

Burke was under no misconceptions as to the type of entertainment she had in mind. Well, why shouldn't he go with her? Dani had made it clear she didn't want him on his terms. Maybe this was the way to purge her from his system. Maybe if he slept with Cynthia, he'd no longer see Dani's face in front of him every time he closed his eyes.

"I'd consider it an honor, Miss James. What time shall I pick you up?"

"Eight o'clock that night will be fine. You can't miss the house. It's the biggest one, right at the end of Front Street. Now I really must go shopping. I need something, well, shall we say, small and lacy, to wear under my dress. I'm sure you understand."

"I understand perfectly. I'll see you then." His eyes followed her as she turned from him, tossed her hair over her shoulder, and casually sauntered down the street. Her hips swayed in an exaggerated side to side motion as she moved.

No doubt about it, Miss Cynthia had a private celebration in mind for New Year's Eve. Burke wondered why he no longer had an appetite as he opened the door to the diner.

          🙣   🙣   🙣

"Dani, are you okay? You don't look so good this morning." Patrick stood in the kitchen doorway and stared at her as if trying to see behind the façade she'd so desperately presented for the last few days.

"I'm fine, just tired." She knew her eyes looked red and swollen again. She'd done her best to hide the results of another sleepless night, but she'd clearly not been as successful as she'd thought.

"Did you and Burke have a fight? Did he do anything to hurt you?" Her brother continued to study her, his mind obviously working overtime trying to understand what was wrong with her.

"We decided not to see each other anymore." She quickly turned away so he couldn't see the pain in her eyes.

Dani didn't know how she'd gotten through the last forty-eight hours. Both Patrick and Shamus had come down the stairs the morning after Christmas Day and known immediately that something was wrong. There was no way she would ever tell them what really happened. Just thinking about it caused her pain, and she knew she would never talk about it with either of them. She just tried to stay busy and as numb as possible.

"That was awful sudden, wasn't it? I mean everything was fine when we left the two of you on Christmas Day." Patrick watched her carefully, as if trying to gauge just how serious this was.

"He won't be around much longer, so we decided there was really no point to keep seeing each other." She couldn't bring herself to call Burke by name. Just thinking his name brought tears to her eyes. Turning away to hide her face from Patrick's concerned eyes, she busied herself wiping down an already clean counter.

Coming up behind her, he gently turned her to face him. "Look at me."

Dani looked up into her brother's familiar face, that was so full of love and concern for her, that the tears she'd tried so hard to hold back started to trickle from the corner of her eyes.

"Did he physically hurt you in any way? Tell me the truth." She could feel the muscles in his arms tense as he waited for her answer. The fury filling his eyes warred with the concern etched on his face.

"No, not physically. I guess I just thought we might have something special. But he was just killing time while he was here." She leaned into him, desperately needing a hug from him and was rewarded when his arms wrapped around her immediately.

"Are you sure, Dani?" His voice was a soft whisper now, as if he was trying to coax the truth from her.

"Yes, he was honest with me if nothing else." Yes, Dani thought, brutally honest. "He didn't want anything serious and, well, I guess I did."

"You love him, don't you?" Patrick asked gently as he released her from his comforting hug.

"Yes, but it's not his problem or your problem. I'll get over it in no time at all." She hoped that her brother believed her, even though she didn't quite believe herself. Sighing, she poured herself a cup of fresh coffee and, without giving it a second thought, automatically took down another mug from the cupboard, filled it, and handed it to him.

"I knew that guy would be trouble from the start." She could hear the harshness in Patrick's voice as he spoke and knew he was blaming himself for not protecting her.

"Promise me you won't make any trouble over this. Please, for my sake. People will talk enough as it is without us adding fuel to the fire."

"I promise I won't go looking for trouble." As he took the cup of coffee she offered him, he reached out and affectionately tugged on her long braid with his free hand. "Why don't you take the day off? Just stay home and take it easy."

Patrick's care and concern for her well being made her feel better about the situation. She knew she wasn't alone as long as she had her brothers.

"No, work is the best thing for me. Besides, you know I'm always booked up Christmas week, cleaning up after people's Christmas parties. It would just give people something else to talk about if I cancelled. Let's get breakfast so I can get out of here before the day is gone." She turned back to the counter and began to cut homemade bread for toast.

෨෨   ෨෨   ෨෨

Picking up her bucket, Dani shuffled to the kitchen. This was the kind of job she liked the best. The house she was cleaning was empty now. The real estate agent had sold it last week, and in two days, the new family would be moving in.

What a wonderful feeling it must be, she thought, *to be starting a new year in a new home with your family.* Not that her life was so bad. She had her own business, two brothers whom she loved very much, and she was young and healthy. She swiped at an errant tear, determined not to let memories of Burke destroy her enjoyment of the house.

She had always been fascinated with the older farmhouses that dotted the landscape around Jamesville. Some people still lived and worked on farms that had been in their families for generations. There were even a couple of apple orchards and a poultry farm. Dani was sometimes sorry that she hadn't been raised on such a farm. But she was a town-dweller whose father had been a truck driver for a local produce wholesaler and her mother had been a full-time homemaker. Not a bad childhood at all, really.

When she took the time to dream, which wasn't often anymore, she found that while many of her dreams had faded, one lived on. Someday, she wanted to close down her cleaning service and try to make a living with her secret hobby.

For years, she'd scribbled and written stories. Stories about a girl who grew up on a farm in a small town and all the adventures she had. They were written for young children and she had five completed and polished manuscripts. She kept meaning to send them out to publishers, but always chickened out or got sidetracked with earning a real living. This year, she was determined to follow through with her dream and try to make it a reality. Even if her stories never got published, at least she would have tried.

As she finished her cleaning and packed up her supplies, Dani admired the kitchen. It was filled with light colored wood and sunshine and was large enough to accommodate a big family with no trouble. She could picture herself here, contently cooking supper or working at a large trestle table, waiting for her family to come home. A picture of Burke popped into her head, and she squeezed her eyes shut to try and dispel the image. It seemed that some dreams just wouldn't die, even when the nail had been hammered into the coffin.

In her mind, she could picture this house complete with furniture and family. Maybe someday, it would be her turn. She smiled a sad little smile as she gathered her things together and let herself out of the house. Locking the door behind her, she decided she would drop the key off to the real estate agency on her way to her final job of the day.

Her mind wandered as she drove down the quiet back road toward town. She thought she was doing fine. Not well, but at least she was getting by. Day by day, she went to work and tried not to think about Burke.

Patrick and Shamus were very supportive and understanding of her mood swings. Sometimes, so much so, that she wanted to scream. It would have been easier if she could have just crawled off somewhere and hid until she felt she could deal with things. Instead she went out into the world each day with a wound that felt as if it was still gaping and bleeding. She'd thought she couldn't hurt any worse. She was wrong.

It was New Year's Eve, and Dani had been surprised to get a call to clean the James house. Everybody knew that they had a live-in maid and a cook. But Cynthia had called in a panic because the staff was too busy with preparations for the New Year's Eve bash, and the house just had to be cleaned because she was expecting a very special guest tonight after the dance was over.

The bedroom was a sea of white with splashes of red. White carpet covered the floor, and pristine linens graced the four poster bed. Red throw pillows were artistically strewn across the bed and the window seat. Two large wardrobes were bursting open with clothes, as was the large walk-in closet. Shoes were lined up and down shelves in the closet, scarves were hung on special hooks, and assortment of skirts, dresses, pants, and sweaters were jammed into every available space. A brass vanity that matched the bed was filled to overflowing with cosmetics and perfumes.

The room hadn't been dirty enough to warrant cleaning, but she cleaned it anyway. It just made her job easier and quicker, and she was glad she would get home earlier than she'd anticipated.

Tonight was the eve of the new year and all Dani wanted to do was go home and bury her head under her own bed covers until it was over. The ache of missing Burke was ever present, but so much more so on a special night, like tonight.

She'd just finished cleaning and polishing the brass fixtures in the bathroom adjoining the bedroom and was packing up her cleaning supplies to leave when Cynthia entered the bedroom, followed by the maid.

"Just lay the dress over there," Cynthia indicated the large bed with a backward flick of her hand. "I do so hope that Burke likes it, I bought it especially for tonight. Where is that sexy little teddy I bought to wear under it?"

"Right here, Miss Cynthia," the maid replied.

Taking the black teddy from the maid, she held it up to herself. "I think he'll like this too." Smiling at herself in the mirror, Cynthia's smiled widened when she saw the movement from the bathroom door.

"Why, Dani, I didn't know you were still here. Maybe I should get your opinion. After all, you and Mr. Black are friends, I believe. Do you think he'll like this?" She turned away from the mirror, still holding the lacy teddy in front of her.

The emotional pain was so crippling at first she couldn't speak. Her throat closed, and no sound would come from it. But then she felt curiously detached from herself, and as if from far away, she heard herself mumble something appropriate to Cynthia. Quickly gathering her things, she fled from the room.

"Goodbye, Dani. Thanks for coming on such short notice." The other woman's voice drifted behind her as Dani bolted down the stairs and out the front door of the house.

Dani had no idea how she got home. She had no memory of driving the truck or entering the house. All she knew was that she was lying on the kitchen floor curled up into a little ball. She'd meant to go to her room, but she'd crumpled as soon as she'd gained the safety of the house. Strangely enough, she didn't shed any tears. For now, she was too numb with pain.

She knew now why Cynthia had wanted her to clean the house. The other woman had planned that little performance well. Up until then, Dani hadn't realized that in the back of her mind she still harbored the belief that Burke would come back to her and admit that he was wrong and that he loved her. Now all hope was gone because it was obvious that he had already moved on to another woman.

That was how Patrick found her. Curled on the kitchen floor with her coat and boots still on. He didn't ask any questions as he bent down, lifted her into his strong arms, and carried her upstairs.

As carefully as a parent might tend a distraught child, he tugged off her outer garments until she was in her underwear. He eased her flannel nightgown over her head and tucked her into bed. She trembled from head to foot by the time he finished, so he lay on the bed next to her and pulled her into his arms, holding her so close she could hear the heavy pounding of his heart.

Crooning softly in her ear, he reassured her that he was there for her and that Shamus was there for her too. That they were a family and they would get through this. Dani finally drifted off to sleep, never aware of the dark thoughts that filled Patrick's mind about Burke Black.

ॐ   ॐ   ॐ

The Jamesville Country Club was awash with white lights and the sounds of soft jazz when Burke escorted Cynthia inside. The loneliness of the saxophone washed over him. All week he had wavered back and forth in his mind. Should he cancel? Should he go? He felt worse now than when he had awakened after the accident. Then he had been only physically damaged, but now he felt as if a vital part of him had been hacked off. And the worst thing about it was that he himself had done the hacking.

"Burke, doesn't this place just look gorgeous?" Cynthia tugged on the sleeve of his tuxedo as she looked up at him, bringing his attention back to her.

He knew he wasn't paying her the attention she deserved and tried to pull himself back to the here and now. "The place looks wonderful and you look wonderful too." She really did, he thought objectively. Cynthia was blonde, beautiful, and made no secret of the fact that she wanted him. Why then, did she leave him totally cold when he should be anticipating what would happen when he took her home?

"Why thank you. I must say that my dress was expensive, but I figure I'm worth every penny of it."

Indeed, Burke noted that her designer dress had to have cost several thousand dollars. The soft, draping black fabric molded her body and showed off her figure to perfection. The diamonds at her ears and around her neck sparkled. He knew that most men would love to be in his shoes, standing next to her.

"I'm sure your father thinks so too." Burke knew he shouldn't be sarcastic, but he couldn't help himself. He thought of Dani and how unaffected she was. Material things didn't matter to her. People did. And besides, Dani looked better to him wearing her old sweatshirt than Cynthia did in a designer dress.

Sighing inwardly, he knew he was going to have to call an early end to the night. There was no way he was going to be able to play this farce out for more than a few hours. He would stay because he had asked Cynthia. It was his own fault he was here.

His date watched him as if trying to figure out if he was being sarcastic or complimentary. He figured she had conveniently decided on the latter when she hooked her arm in his. "Come on, Burke, I'll introduce you to the Flints. Alan is the mayor of Jamesville and his wife, Crystal, heads up most of the more prominent social committees."

For the next two hours, he allowed Cynthia to drag him from couple to couple. Introducing him to all the "important" people, as she called them, seemed to be her mission. In between introductions, she coaxed him out onto the dance floor where she filled in all the details on their social and financial positions.

"That's Abel Pierce and his wife, Nettie." Cynthia indicated a well dressed, middle-aged couple sitting at a table off to the right. "That's the same dress she wore last year. I heard rumors of some financial problems, but I didn't think that Nettie would have the nerve to wear the same dress two years in a row. Why, I'd just die. Apparently, she's put on some weight since last year too. She looks like she barely squeezed into that dress this year."

Burke's patience finally ran out, and his temper flared. He'd had enough. Enough of dancing, enough socializing with all these people he didn't even know, and more than enough of listening to Cynthia's cutting remarks about all the other guests.

"Where do I stand in the scheme of things, Cynthia?" Burke asked Cynthia as he seated her at a small table in the corner of the ballroom.

"Whatever do you mean, Burke?"

"Well, I have no social or financial standing in this community, so where do I stand in the town hierarchy?"

"Really, Burke, you do ask silly questions."

He knew he was making her nervous as she smoothed a nonexistent wrinkle out of her dress and turned to him with a practiced smile upon her face.

"Really, Cynthia. Are you by any chance slumming with me?" He might have found the whole thing amusing if he had been in a better frame of mind. But he had discovered tonight that Miss Cynthia had a malicious streak in her and took great pleasure in cutting other people down.

"I have no idea what you mean. And you have no right to talk to me in this fashion." She pouted prettily and allowed a tear to come to her eye.

"Well, just so you know, I'll be taking you home now and then I'll be going home myself. I don't fancy any extra entertainment tonight."

Cynthia's pout disappeared immediately and a hard gleam entered her eye. She went from flirty and soft to calculating and cruel in the blink of an eye.

"Oh, I suppose you only fancy extra entertainment with those of your own social level, like say Dani O'Rourke." A sly smiled appeared on her face when she noted his surprise.

Burke grew still, his face appeared as if it had been hewn from granite, and the fire in his eyes could have burned even hell. "Leave Dani out of this. If you're a smart little girl, you'll just count your losses and accept them."

Cynthia stiffened slightly, but was apparently past all caution. "Your little friend knows you'll be with me tonight. I made that perfectly clear when she was cleaning my house today. I made sure she knew it was for all night too. It wasn't much fun though, because she barely reacted at all. Just packed up her dust rags and left."

"Miss James, I hope that I never have to set eyes on you again after this moment. And you had better hope that you haven't hurt Dani, or I'll make sure you pay. Good night. I'm sure you'll find some fool to escort you home." Pushing away from the table, Burke walked away from her without sparing a single backward glance.

Impatient now, he didn't wait for the parking attendant, but strode off into the dark parking lot. His truck was easy to pick out in a sea of sedans and sports cars. It was also parked in the far end of the lot. Burke was chilled as he climbed into his truck, and he turned the heat up as soon as he started the engine. As he left the country club behind him, he automatically drove toward the little house on Peach Street.

He couldn't go on like this. It hadn't escaped his notice that he was willing to punish anyone who hurt Dani, yet he knew he had hurt her worse than anyone. He could only hope that she would accept his apology and his explanation. Burke had come to the hard realization that a life with Dani in it, in any capacity, was better than a life without her. He would beg her forgiveness and take whatever she offered, even if it was only ever friendship.

He had missed all the special qualities that defined Dani. The way she cared about people, the way she laughed, and the way she loved. She had brought him into her special circle and he had been touched by the magic.

"Magic," he muttered aloud. That was never as clear as it had been tonight when he had been with Cynthia. Dani didn't care that people had no money or social position. Who they were was more important than what they were. And it had scared him so much that he'd covered his fear with anger. Anger at Dani, at himself, and even at poor Cynthia, who was what she was. It wasn't his place to judge Cynthia, when he hadn't made such great choices in his own life lately.

Dani was what he had been looking for his whole life. Dani was a sense of belonging. A sense of home. Burke knew he had been afraid to believe for fear he would lose it. So, fool that he was, he had thrown it away. This was indeed a true test then. For if she really loved him, maybe he wasn't too late. Maybe he could win her love back and then he would hold it tight and never let it go.

Maybe, just maybe.

Chapter Seven

Standing outside Dani's front door, he shivered as the cold night air penetrated his light tuxedo jacket. For the first time since he was a child, he was afraid.

"How the mighty have fallen," he muttered. Burke Black, millionaire, business tycoon, was afraid. Afraid that he had lost one longhaired, smiling beauty that for one shining moment he had been able to call his own.

He had no experience with love. He had no idea if it would be forgiving or if Dani would withhold it, knowing he now valued it. Maybe she would bargain with it. He knew she didn't seem like the type who would do this, but that was before he had hurt her. Now the rules had changed. All he knew was that he would meet whatever price she asked to have her back again.

Determined as never before in his life, he raised his hand and knocked upon the front door. After waiting a few seconds, he pounded again. Harder.

Maybe she wasn't home. Perhaps, she had gone out to celebrate with another man. The thought of another man touching her smooth skin, kissing her soft lips, made his stomach churn. He was so immersed in his own thoughts that he barely registered the fact that the front door was opening. He glanced up just in time to see the fist that struck his right eye.

"You scum. You've got some nerve showing up here." The smile Patrick gave him was lethal. "But I'm glad you did."

Burke grabbed onto the stair railing, barely managing to keep himself from tumbling down the front steps. Gingerly touching his eye, he knew he would have a shiner tomorrow, but for now his face was blessedly growing numb. Getting past Patrick was the first step in his quest to winning another chance with Dani. He wasn't sure what to say or do, so he spoke from the heart.

"I deserve that and more. And if you want to beat the life out of me, after you listen to me, I won't stop you." Bracing himself on the bottom step, he watched Patrick warily.

"I don't think you'll have a choice in the matter. Nothing you can say will make up for what my sister has gone through in the last week." Standing tall in the doorway with his fists clenched at his sides, Patrick blocked any attempt Burke might have made to enter.

"You might not believe me, but I've been hurting as much as Dani." Burke jammed his hands in his pants pockets, as much to keep them warm as to assure the much younger man that he wasn't a physical threat.

"Somehow I don't think that a date with Cynthia James proves great pain on your part. All it does is show you have no taste." Patrick's disdain was evident in every word he spoke.

"Believe me, accepting her invitation was a reflex reaction to deny the pain I was feeling. I come from a world where everything I have is bought and paid for by me. Dani was a treasure I didn't recognize when I had her."

"So now you think you can waltz in here and take her back?" Patrick glared down at him, all the anger of the last week blazing from his eyes. "I don't think so." Burke could tell the other man was moments away from exploding again.

"No. I know I can't go back, but I want anything Dani is willing to give me."

"She wants nothing to do with you..." Patrick started to move toward Burke as he spoke.

"Patrick." Dani's soft voice cut him off in mid-sentence, stopping him dead in his tracks. "Maybe we should continue this inside."

"You don't have to talk to him if you don't want to." Turning, he wrapped his arm protectively around his sister as he spoke.

"Yes, I do. If this is ever to be finished, I have to hear what he has to say. Come in, Burke." Dani spoke without looking at him, turned, and headed for the living room.

Burke stared at Patrick until he reluctantly moved from the front door.

"I'm warning you, Black, hurt her any further and you'll regret it." Patrick's knuckles were white as he held the front door open.

"I already do, Patrick. You'll never know how much."

Stepping past Patrick, Burke headed to the living room. His whole future depended on the next few minutes. He realized now that a life without Dani would be the same empty, cold life he had been leading for years. Except now, he would know what was missing. He really didn't know if he could live without it, now that he had found it.

"Patrick, will you please leave us alone to talk?" Dani's soft voice cut through Burke's thoughts like a knife, bringing him back to the task at hand.

"If that's what you want. But I'll be in the kitchen. You call if you need me, okay?" Patrick had positioned himself next to his sister like an avenging angel, his fists clenched, ready to defend her.

Reaching out, she grasped her brother's hand. He slowly unclenched it and clasped her fingers tightly for a brief second before he let go. "Thank you," she said as she slowly sank down onto the sofa. Burke watched the interaction between the brother and sister, feeling very much the outsider that he was.

When Patrick finally left the room, Dani finally raised her eyes and looked at him. Burke felt as if all the breath had left his body. Her beautiful eyes that had always sparkled with such light and love were now empty. Empty, that is, except for the pain.

Falling to his knees in front of her, he gazed up at her bleak features. "What have I done to you? Oh God, what have I done?" He buried his face in her lap and shuddered as he brought himself back under control.

It was all over. He had lost her. There was no way she would take him back. And why would she? She had given him something infinitely precious and he had flung it back at her as if it had no value at all. He didn't deserve her, but he would be damned if he would give her up without a fight. His arms tightened their hold around her waist as if by strength alone he could bind her to him.

Then he felt it. At first, he thought if must be a delusion of his brain brought on by the chaos he felt inside him, but then he felt it again. Her hand, ever so lightly touching his hair. Stroking his head. Pulling back, he raised his head and stared up at her.

"Dani, please listen to me. Let me explain everything to you. Give me that chance." He stared into her eyes as if by shear will alone he could get her to give him a chance to win her back.

"What do you have to say that is so different from the last time you were here? Am I now worth more than short-term lust, as you called it? Do I still have value in dollars and cents? Am I cheaper than Cynthia? Is that why you're here?" Every sentence was uttered in a flat monotone voice. She had forgotten nothing he had said. He had much to answer for.

A pain burned deep inside his chest. "How could I have said those things to you?" He wanted to grab her and hold her tight, but instead, he carefully placed his hands on her shoulders and gently squeezed them. She held herself so still, as if one false word or move from him could shatter her. "Don't you dare compare yourself to Cynthia. She's not fit to be in the same room with you. Give me a chance, Dani."

"A chance for what, Burke?"

Sliding his hands down over her arms, he carefully grasped her much smaller hands in his. "Look at me, Dani."

She looked down into his face and drew in a quick breath to steady herself. He didn't know if she would ever be able to bring herself to trust him again, let alone admit to loving him.

He automatically tightened his grip on her, needing the physical contact.

"I've never met anyone like you before. I know I told you I sold my business but I never told you why."

She looked totally confused by his abrupt change of subject. Her brows drew together in a perplexed frown. "I don't understand."

"I know you don't, honey, but I'll try to explain."

"I thought it was because of the accident."

"In a roundabout way, it was. You see, when I woke up in the hospital, I was forced to look at my life. I was alone. I had built a business and financial security, but for what? The only visitors I had were business associates who needed my signature or good will."

"Oh, Burke." Pulling her right hand from his grasp, she gently cupped his scarred cheek, caressing it with her fingers.

Burke recaptured her hand, lightly kissed it, and held it tight. "I'm not telling you this because I want your pity. I want you to understand what my world was like. I had a home and business but no real life. I knew I had to change things, so I sold my business and house, and came out here to think. Then I met you."

"Yes, and then you met me," Dani echoed softly. She was watching his face carefully, searching for what, he wasn't sure. She was like a wild creature, held by him, not by his grip on her, but by her loving nature and her compassion for him.

"You were unlike anyone I've ever known. When you and your family gave so much to me, I didn't know how to react. I kept waiting for the bottom line. Nothing in my life has ever been free, and I was waiting to see how much this would cost me." He released his hold on her, scrubbed his hands over his face, and pushed his hair out of his eyes. He knew he must look as wild as he felt.

"There are some things money can't buy, Burke, and they're the most important things." Her sad smile told him that she understood where his attitude had come from, but she was at a loss as to how to change it. "Maybe it's best if you go."

"No!" Grabbing her hands, he clung tight to them, only releasing his grip when his knuckles turned white. He automatically rubbed his fingers over her hand, hoping to soothe any pain he might have caused her. "I understand that now. Before, I thought you wanted payment for what you gave me and that you wanted more than I would or could pay, physically and emotionally. Now I understand what you were giving to me. Your gift of understanding and acceptance was beyond price, and I was too blind to see it or accept it."

"So where does that leave us, Burke?" She slumped back onto the sofa, and he realized just how physically tired and emotionally worn out she was.

"After what I did, maybe I'm not worth the emotional cost. But do you think we could start over? I won't rush you in any way, Dani. I just want to be with you in whatever way you'll have me." He didn't dare ask if she still loved him. He figured that if he could spend time with her he could convince her to love him again.

"What about Cynthia?" Her blue eyes stared straight into his, demanding an honest answer. She sat on the worn sofa, as regal as any queen, awaiting his answer.

"I only took her out this evening so I could pretend that I didn't hurt. She taunted me about your encounter this afternoon." He was still furious at the mere thought of Cynthia's cruelty. "I left her and came here. If she was a man, I would have hurt her for the pain she caused you."

He shook his head, disgusted with himself. "But I've caused you the most pain, and for that, your brother had every right to slug me. I think I would have been disappointed in him if he hadn't." Reaching up, he gingerly touched his eye, which was starting to swell, and was unable to hold back a small grin. "Well, maybe not too disappointed. Patrick has a wicked left hook."

For the first time, Dani seemed to notice the swelling in his right eye. "You're hurt. We've got to put some ice on that." She tried to rise from her seat on the sofa, but he held her back.

"Dani, honey, I deserve to hurt for what I've done to you. Just look at you, you've lost weight, you've got shadows under your eyes, and your eyes are puffy from crying."

Her smile was self-conscious, and she brushed a stray lock of hair from her face. "You sure know how to make a girl feel beautiful."

"Don't you know that to me you couldn't be more beautiful than you are now? You're beautiful from the inside out. It shines from you like gold, and I'm greedy enough to want it all to belong to me."

"Oh, Burke." A single tear slid down the side of her face. "I didn't think I had any tears left," she tried to joke as she swiped at her face.

Burke closed his eyes at the pain that simple statement brought. "Why don't you yell at me? Rant, rave, and scream! I'd feel better if you did."

"The pain I feel is beyond those things. I don't know if I can trust you." The tears trickled out of the corners of her eyes, falling in earnest as she spoke the truth.

Tugging her from her seat on the sofa, he pulled her down into his lap, locking his arms tight around her. "It's all right, honey. It's all right," he crooned as he rocked them both back and forth on the living room floor. "I'm not asking for anything but a chance. That's all. Give me the time to prove to you that I'm worth loving. I know how to treat such a gift now, and if, in time, you can trust me enough to give it to me again, you won't be sorry."

He would make her trust him no matter how long it took. One of the things that had made him so successful in business was his ability to focus on an idea or concept and find a way to make it work. He was confident that, if he could be a part of Dani's everyday life, he could make her trust him again. There had to be something he could do to restore her faith in him.

Chapter Eight

Her heart thumped so hard against her chest, she was sure Burke could feel its frantic pounding as he held her. She rested her head on his solid warm chest, loving the feeling of security it gave her. His arms tightened around her and she sighed. It was her move next. Should she give him another chance? Did she really have a choice? *No,* her heart answered back.

"Dani, honey, please look at me." Burke gently tilted her face so he could look into her eyes. "Talk to me. Tell me you'll give me another chance."

Dani looked into eyes, deep and black. Eyes that were so very dear to her. She saw the sincerity and the pain in their depths and knew that she had only one real option.

"Please mean what you say, because I don't think I can survive another week like this one." She searched his face, looking for some kind of reassurance.

"I mean it, honey. Anything you want, at your own pace. I just want us to have another chance." Raising his fingertips to her cheek, he gently traced the curve of her face. "We'll take it slower this time and really get to know each other."

"As long as we take things slowly and you know up front that this doesn't mean I'll sleep with you." She covered his hand with hers and turned it over so she could kiss the palm of his hand. "I don't want to be accused of leading you on again."

She was crushed in a breath-stealing embrace before she had even finished speaking. "That's all I want, honey. Just a chance to start over with you. All I want is some of your time. That's all."

For the first time in a week, she was beginning to feel alive again. She really didn't know if she was doing the right thing, but it was the only thing she could do. She still loved him, and if there was a chance for them to work out their problems, she had to take it. This time she would be cautious and sure about Burke's long-term plans before exposing her own heart and emotions. She had to be sure she could trust him before she opened herself up to him again.

She had no idea where their relationship would go from here, but at the moment just being with him was enough. She no longer felt hollow and empty when she held him in her arms. As she pulled away from him, he flinched.

Dani looked at him. Really looked at him for the first time since he came into the house. The right side of his face was turning dark and his eye was swelling shut. "Oh Burke, I forgot your eye. It must hurt something awful." Scrambling out of his lap, she held out her hand. "Come into the kitchen, and we'll get some ice on it."

Burke took her hand as he stood and pulled her into his arms, holding her tight. She felt his lips brush the top of her head. She felt his reluctance to release her as he gave her one final squeeze before stepping back. But he kept hold of her hand as he followed her, as if he didn't want to lose contact with her. They entered the kitchen and came face-to-face with Patrick.

"Well?" Patrick asked her, all the while keeping a watchful eye on Burke.

"Sit down, both of you," she directed as she went to the refrigerator and took two bags of frozen vegetables out of the freezer section. Turning back to the table, she wasn't sure they really needed ice packs as the frozen looks on both men's faces had certainly dropped the room's temperature to subzero.

Sitting at the kitchen table, both men stared at each other. Patrick glared at Burke. Burke had an impassive look on his face, but his black watchful eyes never left Patrick's face.

She quietly went to the kitchen drawer, took out two clean dishtowels and wrapped them around the bags of frozen food. The silence continued as she placed one ice pack against Burke's face and the other on Patrick's left hand. Both men were still.

"Patrick," Dani began softly, waiting patiently until her brother finally took his eyes off Burke and turned his full attention to her. "Burke and I have talked, and we're going to start seeing each other again."

Patrick stared at her as if he was trying to read her mind. "Are you sure he's worth it, Dani, after all he's put you through?" She knew her brother didn't care that Burke sat across the table from him. His only concern was for her.

"We still have a lot to talk about, but yes, I think it's worth it. Don't worry. We're going to take things slowly." Raising the ice pack, she studied his left knuckles. "I don't think anything is broken."

"I don't care if it's broken or not. I only care about you being hurt." He turned to stare at Burke, who shifted uncomfortably in his chair. "I don't know if you're worth a second chance, but I don't think I have a lot of say in the matter. Use it wisely or we'll have a much longer discussion next time." Removing the ice pack, he flexed his hand to emphasize what kind of *discussion* he had in mind.

Burke actually grinned. "I understand, Patrick. And I admire a man who's honest and straightforward." Abruptly Burke's face turned serious. "But I've got a second chance, and I plan to make the most of it. I never meant to hurt Dani or any of you. I have a lot of things from my past that I have to work through, and I'm sorry you got caught up in it." He continued to look the younger man in the eye as he made his point. "I won't knowingly do anything to hurt her again. On that you have my word."

Patrick took a deep breath and exhaled slowly, taking his time before speaking, weighing Burke's words carefully. "All right, you've got your second chance. Although you may not be too sure you want it in the morning." Slowly, he extended his bruised hand across the table. "That eye is really something."

Burke looked at the hand extended to him and carefully took it, giving it one firm shake before he released it. "To tell you the truth, I didn't feel a thing until a few minutes ago. I guess I had more important matters to worry about."

"If you boys are finished working out your difference and won't beat up each other while I'm gone, you can keep those ice packs on while I get the first aid kit from the bathroom." She

N. J. Walters

had stood quietly by while they talked, but the time had come to be practical about their injuries.

They both looked at her as if they would protest but stopped when they saw the annoyed look in her eyes.

"Yes, ma'am," Patrick answered as he placed the ice pack back on his hand.

"Sure thing, honey," Burke answered easily as he smiled at her.

Dani turned and left the kitchen, heading for the bathroom. Honestly, men were such little boys sometimes. But she smiled as she thought of the men she loved, and she was glad that they had come to some kind of agreement between them.

She was smart enough to realize that Patrick could have made all kinds of trouble for her and Burke if he had wanted to. Patrick was concerned about her, and to tell the truth, she was concerned about her too. Her younger brother knew what she had gone through this week, but he had supported her decision regarding Burke. She only hoped she had made the right one, for all their sakes.

     ‽   ‽   ‽

It was two o'clock in the morning by the time Dani and Burke were settled in the living room with steaming mugs of hot chocolate.

She had returned to the kitchen, first aid kit in hand, to the sound of male laughter. Shamus had returned from his friend's house and had found the two men sitting at the kitchen table comparing injuries. Shamus had been aware that she and Burke

102

were no longer seeing one another, but he really hadn't known how much suffering she had gone through. Only Patrick had seen the depth of her pain and helped her through it. Since Shamus was the youngest, both she and Patrick were guilty of trying to protect him as much as possible during times of trouble. It was hard to remember sometimes that he was almost an adult now as well.

"Looks like Patrick helped you and Burke get things straightened out," Shamus had said to her with laughter in his eyes.

"We prefer to call it a gentlemanly discussion," Burke had replied, while trying to keep a straight face. He'd winced in pain when he couldn't quite manage to.

"More like schoolboys," she'd retorted as she had gently rubbed an antiseptic cream around Burke's eye.

From there, both injuries had been tended, and both her brothers had retired upstairs for the night. She knew that Shamus would go to bed thinking that whatever problem had been between her and Burke was fixed. But Patrick would probably stay awake until Burke left, just to make sure she was all right.

Burke took a sip of the hot chocolate and placed his mug on the coffee table. He turned to stare at her by the light of the Christmas tree, which he had plugged in when they had settled in the living room.

"Happy New Year, Dani," Burke said as he continued to look at her. "I can hardly believe I'm really here with you."

"Yes, I guess it is New Year's Day. I forgot about it with everything else that's happened today."

It seemed impossible to her that her life had changed so drastically in a matter of hours. She had gone from the depths of despair to a fragile hope in less than one day. Suddenly, she felt very tired. Happy, but tired.

As if sensing the change in her mood, Burke wrapped his arm around her and pulled her gently onto his lap. "Just relax, honey, and let me hold you. You can't know how amazingly good it feels for me to have you in my arms."

Dani felt her body relax. She didn't seem to have any choice in the matter. It just felt so natural and right to be held by Burke again. It was like coming home. Snuggling closer to him, she placed her hand on his chest and could feel the strong beat of his heart against her palm. "I missed you so much." She said it quietly, as if making some deep dark confession.

"I missed you too, Dani, you'll never know how much." Burke's lips brushed the top of her head as he pulled her even closer. "I'm surprised that you still have your tree up. I'd have thought you would have torn it down the day after our fight."

"I couldn't bear to come into the living room." Dani looked down at her hands, not wanting him to see the pain that she knew was there in her eyes. "There were too many memories in this room. Good memories from when we put the tree up and then the bad memories of what happened Christmas night. I just couldn't bear to be in here."

Slowly, he began to rock her back and forth in his arms. "I'm so sorry for that, but I'm glad you didn't take it down. I'm glad we had a chance to enjoy it again, just the two of us. It's a special tree and not just because it's my first real one, but because I was a part of it with you and your family."

He stared at the tree as if he was trying to memorize every part of it. "No matter what happens from here on, I want you to know you've made a difference in my life and in me. You've changed how I look at the world and at people. It's been a hard time for both of us, but in the long run I think that it's worth it."

"Maybe you can help me take down the tree tomorrow?" She was deeply moved by what he'd said, and like him, she hoped that they would be able to move past their problems and create a future together. Trying to fight back a yawn and losing the battle, she closed her eyes, just to rest them for a moment.

"I'd like that a lot, Dani. I want us to spend more time together. There's so much I want to talk to you about." His own words surprised him, but he knew they were nothing less than the truth. He never talked to anyone about himself or his plans. Never shared his hopes or his dreams. But suddenly, he found he wanted to do just that with Dani. She would understand him and would help him see the future more clearly. He didn't know how he knew this. He only knew it was true.

"What time tomorrow, Dani?" He pushed back a strand of hair that had fallen on her face, loving the feel of her long hair, and took a moment to let the shiny lock glide through his fingers.

When he got no answer, he glanced down and saw that her eyes had closed and her breathing had deepened. His chest tightened, and he suddenly found it hard to breathe. She had trusted him enough to fall asleep in his arms. It was definitely a good beginning.

"I'll take care of you, honey, I promise." He whispered his vow as he sat there in the living room, staring at the Christmas tree, soaking in the peace of the moment. A deep contentment unlike anything he'd ever felt in his life filled him. He continued to run his hands lightly through Dani's hair, careful not to wake her, but needing to keep touching her.

He didn't know how much time had passed when he jerked upright, waking from the light doze he'd fallen into. Shaking off the lure of sleep, he shifted Dani in his arms and stood. She didn't stir except to burrow closer to him, rubbing her cheek against his chest. That simple action made him smile, until the pain from his face made him wince instead.

Taking a deep breath, he inhaled her unique fragrance, part vanilla and something elusively Dani. It was amazing that just holding her made him feel so damn good. His arms tightened protectively around her as he carried her from the room.

As he climbed the stairs with her cradled in his arms, a door opened upstairs, and Patrick appeared on the landing above. "She's asleep," Burke whispered. "Where's her room?"

Turning, Patrick silently led the way into Dani's room, pulled the covers back on her bed, and then moved aside. Burke gently laid her gently on the bed, all the while aware of her brother watching his every move.

He pulled the covers over her, tucking her in tight before leaning down and placing a soft kiss on her lips. Still fully dressed, Dani snuggled deeper under the covers, her exhaustion evident by the faint dark circles under her eyes. "Good night," Burke whispered in her ear. Turning, he left the room with Patrick close behind him.

"Tell Dani I'll be back after lunch tomorrow to help her with taking down the tree." He kept his voice low as Patrick closed her bedroom door.

"I'll tell her."

"Good night then." Burke started down the stairs again. "I'll lock up on my way out." Patrick said nothing, but Burke could feel the other man's eyes on his back, watching him, until the front door clicked shut behind him.

Burke stood outside the front door of the little house on Peach Street and inhaled a deep breath of the crisp winter air. It helped clear the sleep from his head for the ride home. He ambled to his truck, climbed in, and drove away. To help stay alert, he kept the heat on low and tuned into a rock and roll oldies radio station. He hummed along to the music all the way back to the cabin. When he finally fell in bed, he slept deeply and peacefully the whole night through for the first time in a week.

Chapter Nine

The sound of someone moaning dragged Burke from his slumber. It took him a few groggy moments to realize that he was the one actually making the irritating noise. Rolling over in bed, he cautiously touched the side of his face.

"Oh, Lord help me," he muttered as he dragged himself out of bed and down the hall to the bathroom, carefully holding his head in his hands.

Flipping on the overhead light, he winced as the light hit his eyes. Ever so gradually, he raised his head. It was a slow process. The sight that greeted him in the mirror hardly reassured him. Yep, he had one dandy of a shiner all right. His right eye was puffed and swollen, so that he could barely see out of it at all. Maybe his lack of vision was a blessing in disguise. What he saw out of his bloodshot left eye didn't make him feel any better.

The area around his right eye was extremely dark with a smattering of dark purple thrown in. The scar that covered his left cheek seemed redder than usual, as he was a little pale this morning. That, coupled with the fact that he needed a shave and a haircut, made him look more than a little disreputable. He looked like he'd been on an all night bender. It wasn't a pretty sight. He just hoped he hadn't looked quite this bad last night.

Opening the medicine chest, he rooted around until he found a bottle of pain relievers he'd bought at the drugstore last week. Bottle in hand, he made his way to the kitchen, being careful not to bounce off the walls as he walked. His legs were wobbly as he staggered down the short hall. The floor felt cold on his bare feet, but he didn't care. He didn't turn on the light even though it was still dark outside. He didn't think his poor head would survive any more light. All he wanted to do was to get some ice on his face and take a couple of pain pills.

It took him three tries to match up the little arrows on the childproof cap, but he finally managed to pop the top, extract, and swallow three of the little white pills. He ran some cold water into a glass and gulped it down while he leaned against the counter for balance. He rummaged around in the kitchen drawers until he found a clean dishtowel. Taking his time, he pulled some ice cubes from the freezer and wrapped them in the towel, making up a cold pack. That done, he made the trek back to bed.

Piling his pillows carefully under his aching head, he eased himself under the covers. He placed the cold pack on the right side of his face, flinching when the ice made contact with his abused flesh. It took him a few minutes, but when he was finally settled comfortably in bed, he realized that he was no longer sleepy.

Burke's thoughts drifted back to the night before. Patrick sure had a nasty left hook, but that was okay. He was almost sure Patrick would have swollen knuckles this morning, so he considered them even. He hadn't had an eye like this since he was a kid and fighting all those who taunted him about his poverty and promiscuous mother. He let those thoughts drift away, not wanting to think about those days, long gone.

As he lay in bed, nursing his swollen eye and pounding head, Burke contemplated how drastically his life had changed in the last few months. Six months ago, he was a shrewd businessman, always on the look out for the next big deal. Always one step ahead of the competition. That was what had made him so good at making money. He had always been able to read the trends and know where they were headed before anyone else. His last deal had been a company take-over that had netted him a cool fifteen million when he was through dividing the spoils and reselling the pieces.

Summed up like that, his life seemed pretty narrow. In retrospect, he realized that he hadn't really enjoyed his money. Sure he had spent a lot of it on his home and his lifestyle, but he hadn't really taken any pleasure in it. People never seemed to understand that it was the security the money represented, rather than the money itself, that he craved.

No doubt about it, six months ago, any one of his business associates would have said that Burke Black had the world by the tail. He had had it all. Money, power, and women.

Then it had all collapsed.

He had never really remembered all the details of the car crash that had changed his life. The police had told him that a drunk driver had run a red light and slammed into his vehicle as he'd proceeded through the intersection. All Burke could remember was the sudden impact. The knowledge that, suddenly, something was horribly wrong. Then came the pain.

It was the pain he remembered most of all. When he had finally come around, he was lying in a hospital bed with his face and head bandaged and his leg hoisted in a cast and pulley system. By then he welcomed the seemingly unending aching. It let him know he was still alive.

It had been a long three weeks before he was allowed to go home. Weeks filled with constant pain, like a toothache that never ended. His face and his leg were the worst, but in truth his whole body had sported large, ugly, bruises that had covered his legs, chest, arms, and back. It hurt to breathe, and sleep became a luxury that came only after he gave in to the nurses and took something strong enough to deaden the pain. He didn't like having to give in to his weakened body, but was smart enough to know he'd never heal if he didn't sleep.

His days had been filled with challenges. Things he'd taken for granted before. Just taking care of basic human needs was beyond him. He'd hated the fact that the nurses had had to shave and wash him. And the whole bathroom thing was an experience he didn't want to repeat. After the first day, he'd hired a private male nurse, so he didn't have to feel so uncomfortable asking for things that he needed.

Other than sleeping, eating, and following doctor's orders, he hadn't had much to do in the first week. He wasn't able to work right away, and the problem with having that much time on his hands was that there was nothing to do but think. Since Burke had never done anything by half measures, he had thought a lot.

The lack of visitors had brought many truths home to him. Sure, some of his staff had called, and most of his business acquaintances had sent flowers, but he had not had one personal visitor. Only one member of his staff had come by and that was because Burke had requested it. It was a sad thing for a man to wake up at the age of thirty-five and realize that he had no friends. Even Scrooge had had Marley. Or at least Marley's ghost.

Examining his life with an objective eye, if one can have an objective eye from a hospital bed, he had not liked what he had discovered. His life was extremely limited, very dull, and filled with an excess of shallow people. People much like himself, or rather, as he had been. Every day he was changing from the driven man he'd been.

He couldn't quite figure out where his life had gone so wrong. He had always set goals for himself, and he had attained them. But somehow he hadn't ended up where he had envisioned himself.

When he thought back to his childhood dreams, he admitted to himself that he had attained most of them. Growing up in an overcrowded and often uncaring big city, he had wanted the financial security that he had never had. He wanted a home that no one could take from him, enough food to eat, good clothes to wear, and money in his pocket. All of this, he had attained. What he hadn't foreseen was his own loneliness.

Deep inside, he also had another dream. One he hadn't allowed himself to think about in a long, long time. It was the dream of a family. His family. People who would care about him, a wife who would love him, and children. Children he would watch grow up. And he would love them as he hadn't been loved in his childhood. Most people didn't know how eager children were to love and be loved, but he did, and he wanted that kind of love with a fierce longing. The details of this dream hadn't mattered as much as the feeling it brought him. He wanted the security of his own family. Somewhere along the years, this dream had gotten lost in the gritty everyday reality of building a financial empire.

This was the biggest source of his discontent when he had awakened after the accident. If he had died, what would have happened to all he had built? He had no family to leave it to. It would have been divided between charities after the government had taken its chunk. He had more than enough to live well for the rest of his life. So what was he making all the money for?

It was then and there that he had made the life-changing decision to sell it all and go away for awhile. He'd wanted to find somewhere quiet to rethink his life. He laughed out loud at the thought. Quiet. His life had been anything but quiet since his first meeting with Dani. If anything, for the first time in years, he felt alive.

Life was strange sometimes. Never in a million years would he have thought that something this good could come out of something as horrible as that accident. That aside, he never thought he'd be happy to have a black eye either, but he was. The shiner was a sign that he had a second chance with Dani and a second chance at maybe fulfilling some of his dreams.

Dani and her family were slowly changing him. At first he resisted it, comfortable with his cynicism and his loner ways. At home with being the way that he always had been. He found himself evolving, keeping those parts of him that still served him, but opening himself enough to grow as well. Just the fact that Dani's feelings mattered to him was a revelation. It meant he really was changing. And change, no matter how much we may want it, is never comfortable.

Burke opened his eyes slowly. He was feeling more like himself now. Not great, but he would live. The sun was just starting to come up, and he was suddenly glad to just be alive.

If being in business had taught him one thing, it was to take advantage of his opportunities. With that in mind, he figured he had time to take a shower, then head over to Dani's and take her out for a New Year's Day breakfast. That is, if he could find somewhere open in Jamesville on New Year's Day.

❧   ❧   ❧

Dani rested in bed, tucked under her down-filled comforter, and watched the sun come up. How different from yesterday this day was dawning. If she hadn't awoke still fully dressed, she might have thought that she had dreamed it all.

She still had a hard time believing that the man in the rumpled tuxedo last night was Burke. It was almost surreal that he had turned up just past the stroke of midnight on New Year's Eve, ready to fight if necessary, in order to get a second chance with her. It was like something out of a romance novel. Things like that didn't happen to ordinary people like her.

Yet it had.

Burke had come to her on bended knee and apologized for everything he had said and done. He had easily passed off the punch Patrick had thrown. Nothing had seemed to matter to him last night, but her.

Dani sighed. Maybe she was an idiot, but she couldn't give up. She wouldn't. She loved Burke, for better or for worse, and she had already been through the *for worse* part. Dani also knew she couldn't go through that again. She would give him a second chance, but this time she would proceed with caution. They would take things slowly. Burke had agreed to this, and she had taken him at his word.

Life was strange and could change in a single moment or with a chance encounter. It was ironic that Cynthia had been not only the cause of their first meeting, but had also played a part in their problems. Dani and Cynthia had lived in the same town their whole lives, but their lives had really never intersected before.

A few weeks ago, she was happy in her life with her work and her family. Maybe it wasn't perfect, but she had been content. Now her dreams stirred in her head. Dreams from her childhood. Dreams of a husband and a home and family. Dreams she thought she had put to rest. Or had she just let them die?

Only time would tell what would happen between her and Burke, but she cautiously allowed herself to hope. And with each moment of hope, her dreams taunted her. Maybe, she thought, maybe a life filled with a husband and children would come true. It was a good way to start the New Year. It was a

N. J. Walters

time for hopes and dreams. It was, indeed, a time of new beginnings.

Her only regret from last night was that she didn't remember Burke carrying her up to bed. He must have or she would still be downstairs on the sofa. It could have been Patrick, but she didn't think so. She had a vague memory of being carried, and the arms around her had felt like Burke's.

She didn't know when he left, but he had held her until she had fallen asleep. That she was sure of. Her last conscious memory was of being held in Burke's lap as they talked. The secure feeling of being held tight in his arms, the smell of his cologne in the air, the feel of his suit jacket against her cheek, and the murmur of his voice in her ear.

Dani smiled. It was time to rise and shine. With any luck, Burke might find his way over here for breakfast. If not breakfast, then definitely supper. Either way, she needed to get a shower and wash away the grubby feeling that came from sleeping in her day clothes.

She was still smiling when she stepped under the hot shower spray. Yes indeed, this was a good way to start the New Year.

Chapter Ten

The month of January passed in a blur of happiness for Burke. Dani and her family constantly amazed him. They had promised him a second chance, and they delivered. There had been no snide remarks about what he had done and no sly innuendoes that he owed them for the hurt he had caused.

He had returned to the O'Rourke house the next morning with the intention of taking Dani out to breakfast at Jessie's Diner. Instead, he had eaten bacon, eggs, and homemade biscuits, all cooked to perfection by Dani. Later that day, he had joined the family as they dismantled the Christmas tree. To his delight, taking down the tree was as enjoyable as erecting it had been.

It was both fascinating and amusing to watch the family interacting with one another. Dani bossed the boys around, directing them on what to put where and admonishing them to be careful. Patrick and Shamus just rolled their eyes and laughed while carrying out their assigned roles. It quickly became obvious that the good-natured teasing and taunting were as much a part of the yearly ritual as the packing away of the decorations was. Burke found that he laughed along with them as they removed ornaments and wrapped them under Dani's watchful eyes.

While Patrick dragged the tree out to the curb for the town council to pick up later in the week for recycling, he and Shamus muscled the boxes back into their storage space for another year. Dani was a whirlwind of vacuuming and dusting until everything was back to normal in the living room. They'd spent the afternoon watching an old movie on the television while sneaking peaks at the various football games.

They finished the evening with a vegetable casserole and a vegetable salad. When Patrick asked if they were turning vegetarian, Dani had just laughed and said that she had recently come into a large supply of formerly frozen vegetables. They had all laughed then. No further reference was made to the disagreement between Burke and Patrick. They had all put it behind them and were ready to build on their tentative truce.

ॐ   ॐ   ॐ

Since then, he had spent as much time with Dani in the last month as he could. She was back to her regular schedule of work, and he had to spend so much time every day keeping track of his investments and his money. That was a habit he wasn't going to break. He still wanted to make the most of his money until he decided what he wanted to do next with his life.

They were learning things about each other in every moment they spent together. Couple things. He had recently discovered that Dani hated nuts of any kind, and yet she liked smooth peanut butter. She now knew that he hated nutritious cereals but had a weakness for the sugarcoated kind. For the first time in his life, Burke was actually dating. The kind of dating one usually did in high school or college, and the kind he had missed.

He found himself doing things he had never done before. The O'Rourke family had taken him to a local hockey game. He had never followed the sport, but found himself enjoying the action. The most fun had been watching Dani as she screamed and shouted with the rest of the fans when her team scored or the referee made a call against them. She looked so cute wearing her team jersey, and he cuddled her to keep her warm. They shared steaming French fries and ice cold sodas and returned home in triumph as their team won by a score of six to two.

The people from his old life would never have recognized this Burke Black. The man they had known had been tough, cold, and ruthless. His only concerns in life had been making money and ensuring that no one could get close enough to him to hurt him in any way. This new Burke Black actually smiled and laughed, and although he was still making money, it was no longer the sole focus of his life.

Dani was a big part of his life now, and she had the power to make him happy or to hurt him. Emotionally, she was closer to him than he had ever allowed anyone to be. Sometimes the whole idea of giving someone else that kind of power over him scared him, but the alternative, a life without Dani, was more frightening.

Although their time together had been wonderful, always lurking in the back of his mind was their past. They had never discussed what had happened on or before New Year's Eve. It was if they had decided to wipe the slate clean and start over, and neither one of them wanted to upset their tentative new happiness by bringing up the past.

Burke had seen Cynthia around town once or twice, and every time he saw her, he wondered how strong was the bond he and Dani were building. Could their relationship survive another test? He wasn't sure. He also knew that these thoughts, though unspoken, had passed through Dani's mind as well. The look she got in her eye sometimes when someone mentioned Cynthia in casual conversation. They both had worries, but both were trying hard to live in the now and hopefully build a long-term relationship.

"How did Shamus do in his math test?" Burke asked Dani as she slid into a comfortable corner booth at Jessie's Diner.

It was the first time he had taken her out to dinner, as she usually insisted that they eat at the O'Rourke house. They all took turns cooking, and even he had tried his hand at it. But he had finally insisted on taking her out to eat. It marked a new stage in their relationship.

They certainly hadn't been hiding the fact that they were seeing each other, but there was something about dining out together for the evening meal that had people looking at them like they were a couple. Dani knew that people watched their every move, while pretending not to.

"He did well, actually. He got an eighty-five, thanks to the help you've given him." Dani settled herself onto the red vinyl, cushioned seat and smoothed her sweater in a nervous gesture.

It was ridiculous to be nervous about dining with Burke at Jessie's, but she was. She was a little afraid of what people might say about them. She tried not to be affected by gossip, but she remembered all too well what it was like to be the topic on everyone's tongue. When her mother had passed away, many had thought that the boys needed to go into foster care and that Dani, as a young girl of eighteen, wouldn't be able to handle two young boys.

Their major concern had been Patrick. He'd started hanging around with a wild crowd just after their father had died, but their mother had refused to see the problem. Patrick had started skipping school, coming home late, and sneaking cigarettes. He had been headed for trouble.

Dani had been the one to sit down with him before their mother's funeral and lay it on the line for Patrick. The government officials would let them stay together as long as there were no problems. One sign of skipping school or causing problems and they would be split up, regardless of what they all wanted. She was never sure if her brother was scared or just starting to grow up, but things had changed from that moment forward. Patrick had been a godsend to her from then on.

Dani's thoughts were interrupted when the waitress came to the table.

"Good evening, Burke. Dani." Shannon Brooker handed them their menus as she spoke. "The soup today is beef and barley, and the special is macaroni and cheese. Would you like anything to drink?"

"I'll just have water, Shannon," she answered.

"I'll have a coffee."

"Okay, I'll get your drinks and be back to take your order in a minute."

Dani watch the waitress walk away and then turned back to Burke. "How does Shannon know who you are?" Dani realized in a flash that it was really none of her business and that she was acting like a jealous wife. "Forget it, it's none of my business."

"Actually, I eat a lot of breakfasts here. I like to come in after my morning walk." He smiled as he answered as if amused by her show of possessiveness. "That and the fact that I make lousy coffee."

"Oh." Feeling silly, she buried herself behind her menu before she made any more stupid remarks. Honestly, she didn't know what was wrong with her tonight.

Jessie's was an old-fashioned diner. The tables were covered with red-checkered clothes and matched the curtains that hung in the windows. The booth seats and chairs were covered in red vinyl that creaked and groaned when sat on. The napkins were stuffed into a metal dispenser at each table and sat alongside the salt, pepper, ketchup, and vinegar bottles.

The booth in which they sat was one of eight that lined the window side of the diner. There were also eight tables and a dozen stools along the counter that were favored by the truckers who came to Jessie's. But it wasn't the old-fashioned decor that kept Burke and everyone else coming back. It was the food. While the fare was ordinary burgers and fries, soups, and casseroles, it was delicious and there was always plenty of it. That, coupled with the economical cost and the friendly service, kept the business thriving from the time it opened at six in the morning until it closed at nine in the evening.

"So how does Shannon know you?" Burke was smiling at her when she lowered her menu to look at him. When she saw him smiling, she felt something inside her start to relax. This was just plain silly. She had no reason to be nervous.

"Actually, Shannon is Jessie's niece. She's been hanging out here for as long as I can remember. I don't know where her parents are, but she's lived with her aunt since she was little. She started waiting tables while she was in high school and kept it up when she graduated last year.

Just then the tall red-haired girl under discussion returned to the table and deftly placed two glasses of water, Burke's cup of coffee, and cream and sugar in front of them. "Are you ready to order yet?"

"Dani, what would you like?"

"I think I'll have the special, I love macaroni and cheese, especially Jessie's." Her stomach rumbled as she handed the menu back to Shannon.

Burke laughed when she slapped a hand over her stomach. She knew her face was as red as the ketchup bottle, but he didn't make any comment. Instead, he studied his menu and placed his order. "I'll have the hamburger platter, with fries. If I'm going to eat the hamburger I might as well go all the way. Make it with the works."

"You got it." Shannon wrote down their orders, collected Burke's menu, and headed toward the kitchen.

Dani was just about to speak when she saw a familiar figure hurrying toward them. She sighed. The inquisition was about to begin.

"Don't look now, but we're about to be invaded." Dani smiled at the short grandmotherly looking woman with curly gray hair and sharp blue eyes. "Good evening, Mrs. Woods. How are you this evening?"

"Evening, Dani. This the young man you bought one of my sweaters for?"

She could see very well that he was wearing the sweater that Dani had bought from her, but Mrs. Woods obviously wanted an introduction. She might be an older widow woman, but she was still sharp enough to know this could be serious. She had also been a close friend of Dani's Grandmother O'Rourke, and she obviously felt she owed it to her old friend to keep an eye on her grandchildren.

"Yes, Mrs. Woods. This is Burke Black. Burke, Mrs. Woods."

Burke, who had risen when the older woman had first spoken, held out his hand. "It's a pleasure to meet you ma'am. You do beautiful work." He glanced down at his sweater as she took his hand in a firm grip and then released it.

"Sit down, boy, sit down. I don't aim to stay. I just wanted to see who was keeping company with Dani. I must say, you look fit enough. Well, I'll be on my way, Shannon's coming with your supper." She nodded at Dani and winked. "I'll see you later this week." With that, she turned and left.

With a bewildered look on his face, Burke watched her hurry over to the far side of the diner and join a group of older ladies who were already settled into a booth. Mrs. Woods turned and gave Burke a little wink and a wave before she sat down next to her friend and started talking immediately. Unable to help herself, Dani burst out laughing just as their dinner arrived.

Shannon placed the plates of steaming hot food in front of them, a knowing smile on her face. "His first time?"

"Yes," Dani managed to reply between laughs.

Shannon gave Burke a look of sympathy before hurrying back to the counter.

"Who was that whirlwind? She actually called me *boy*." He shook his head in wonder.

"She's a wonderful woman, but she does love to gossip. She's never mean about it, but she likes to keep on top of what's happening here in Jamesville. She knows everything about everyone." She had also been Dani's first private customer for her cleaning business. Dani had never figured out if she was being generous or if she was hoping Dani would have gossip to share from the other places she was cleaning. If that was the case, she must have been disappointed, because Dani never talked about her customers. But she was still cleaning Mrs. Woods' home all these years later.

They relaxed and dug into their supper. The conversation was light as they each talked about their day. Dinner was delicious and for a while only the sound of utensils scraping plates could be heard. It was a comfortable silence that didn't need to be filled with mindless chatter.

Dani found that once she relaxed, she enjoyed herself. She had only been taken out to eat a few times in her life and that was a long time ago, when she had still been in high school. She had eaten at Jessie's many times with Patrick and Shamus, but this was different. It was so pleasant to share a meal with someone you cared about. *Someone you loved*, she corrected herself. For she knew she still loved him. She only wished he would open up about himself a bit more. *One step at a time*, she admonished herself. And, indeed, they had taken many steps such as this one since New Year's Day.

Shannon finished clearing the table and poured a second cup of coffee for Burke and a first cup for Dani. "Thanks, Shannon," Burke said as she left their table. "Don't look now, but the law is almost on us."

Dani looked over her shoulder as Burke spoke, and smiled at the large, uniformed man, with the shrewd brown eyes and endearingly homely face, heading in their direction. "Hello, Sheriff Tucker," she greeted him as he stopped by their table.

"Evening, Dani." He smiled as he laid a large hand on her shoulder and gave it a quick squeeze. "How are you doing?"

"I'm fine. How are you and Mrs. Tucker?"

"We're fine. Emma was saying just the other day that she hasn't seen you in a couple of weeks."

"I've been a little busy, but tell her I'll call her this week." She looked at him quizzically, wondering why he'd really stopped at their table. Mrs. Tucker knew that Dani would be contacting her soon about working on the upcoming spring fair.

"That I will." The sheriff turned his steely gaze on Burke. "I heard from Mrs. Woods that you were having dinner with our Dani here, and I thought I should come and check you out."

Dani figured that Burke should be used to the plain, blunt speech of the citizens of Jamesville. You knew where you stood, even if you didn't always like the place you were standing. It was one of the reasons she liked living here, but it still took her by surprise every now and again. She watched him, curious to see how he'd respond.

"Burke Black." He held out his hand as he stood and waited to see if the sheriff would take it.

"Albert Tucker," he replied as he shook Burke's hand. "Dani's father was a good friend of mine. Yep, Patrick O'Rourke and I go back a long ways together. I wouldn't take kindly to anyone who would hurt his little girl, if you know what I mean." He gave Burke a pointed look.

"I know what you mean, Sheriff, and I'm glad that Dani's had someone looking out for her for all those years before I got here. But I'm here now, if you know what I mean." Burke put a lot of emphasis on the last part of his statement.

For a long moment, the sheriff stared at the man standing patiently waiting in front of him, and then he smiled. "I think you'll do just fine, son. Well I got to get going. Emma will have my head if I'm late tonight. We got company coming. See you later, Dani. Burke." The last was said as he gave Dani one last pat on her shoulder. Seemingly satisfied for now, the older man turned and left them alone, nodding and speaking to other people on his way out the door.

Dani just sat there, utterly speechless. Her cheeks felt like they were on fire. She knew for sure now that everyone had been checking them out tonight. It was embarrassing for a woman her age to have so many obvious chaperones.

"I'm sorry, Burke, I had no idea it was going to be like this." She finally managed to pull her thoughts together to speak.

Burke had calmly retaken his seat, picked up his coffee cup, and taken a sip as if nothing had happened. "Nobody has any right to question you like this."

"It's okay, honey," Burke answered gently. "You don't know how lucky you are to have so many people who care enough to be worried about you."

She thought back to the few comments he had made about his childhood and knew it hadn't been a happy one. "Burke, when are you going to tell me about yourself, about your past?" In spite of her resolve not to push things, Dani couldn't help herself. She wanted to know everything about him. No, she needed to know what had made him the man he was today.

He watched her carefully, as if searching her expression for something. What she wasn't sure, but whatever he saw in her expression made him close his eyes and sigh deeply before he responded to her question.

"Not here. There are too many interruptions. How about a walk down by the river?"

Dani knew that this would be the first time that they would be really alone since they had started seeing each other again. It was time to give him some of her trust.

"I'd like that."

Burke rose from the table, helped her put on her coat, and grabbed his own. He flung several large bills on the table, more than enough to cover supper and a generous tip, and escorted her out to his truck.

Chapter Eleven

The silence in the truck on the drive to the river was emotionally charged and not the comfortable one they had shared over supper. Both of them were aware that their relationship was about to change in a big way, and there was no going back if they wanted to have any kind of future together. Their fears and anxieties about their coming talk kept them company during the short drive.

Usually Dani found the river to be a soothing companion. She especially liked to walk along its banks to where it met the lake. There was a large flat rock at the point where the two merged, and she had always found it a good place to sit and think. She hadn't been there since she'd met Burke, and she had missed it.

The river had been strictly off limits when they had been having problems, as it was located not far from the Cozy Cabins. The last thing she'd wanted then was to run into Burke. It seemed only fitting that they end up here to be alone and share confidences.

Burke glanced at her and then quickly turned his attention back to the road. He didn't have any idea what she was thinking, but she knew he felt the tension as much as she did. His knuckles were white where he gripped the steering wheel as he pulled the truck off the road.

"Damn it, Dani, this is ridiculous." He parked the vehicle and turned off the ignition, his actions as abrupt as his words.

"I know it is." It was a measure of their newfound closeness that they both knew what the other one was talking about.

"Let's walk." He suddenly pushed open the door of the truck, got out, and then slammed it shut behind him.

Dani opened her door more slowly and slid to the ground, unsure if she should approach him. He stood in front of the truck, staring up at the night sky, as if all the answers could be found there. Quietly, she closed her door and walked toward him.

"We don't have to talk about this if it upsets you that much. We can wait until you're ready." She spoke softly, not wanting to disturb his thoughts. She didn't touch him, as he seemed very remote at the moment. Somewhere very far away from her.

"No, it's not that, Dani. It's just...I've never talked to anyone about my childhood before. Not that I have any deep dark secrets. My life has been no better or no worse than anyone else's has. It's just mine, and I've never been one for sharing." Shoving his hands in his jacket pocket, he continued to stare out into the night sky.

"Let's walk on the river path." She held her hand out to him.

Burke stared at her gloved hand for a long moment. The tension grew thicker, but she refused to withdraw. Slowly but surely, he removed his hand from his pocket, reached out, and clasped her hand gently in his.

She led him down the clearly marked path, and they started walking alongside the gurgling river. Pockets of ice had filled parts of the river, but it still ran freely and quickly. The air was crisp, but not too cold for late January, and the stars were shining brightly in the sky even though it was only about eight o'clock. Their boots crunched the thin layer of snow in a constant scrunching sound. That, and the sound of running water, were the only sounds to be heard.

"My mother was an alcoholic who never wanted children." Burke spoke in low tones, keeping his voice hushed, as if he didn't want to disrupt the tranquility of the night.

His voice shook her out of her thoughts, and although she was utterly appalled by what he'd said, she said nothing, waiting for him to speak again. She knew he would find it easier to talk if she didn't ask any questions but just listened to what he had to say.

"My mother and father were never married, as far as I know. My father was just some guy she slept with." He continued to walk for another minute without speaking. "Maybe she didn't even know who the father was. Maybe she just didn't want to say. Anyway, there is no father listed on my birth certificate." He continued to stare off into the night sky as he spoke. Not once did he even glance in her direction.

Dani squeezed his hand lightly in encouragement, but held her silence.

"I guess she did the best she could to raise me. Even in my earliest memories, she was always drunk and angry, and there was never enough food to eat. That never changed over the years."

It took all her restraint not to throw her arms around him and hug him tight. Her heart felt as if it might break. She could easily picture him as a frightened, hungry little boy wanting his mother's love, but never getting it. She wanted to hold him tight and promise that she would never leave him, but she was afraid to break the spell. She also knew he would reject anything he perceived as pity on her part.

"We moved a lot when I was a kid. We kept getting kicked out of our apartment because she drank the rent money." Burke bent down and picked up a stone from the bank of the river. He held it in his hand as if weighing it, before he fired it into the depths of the running river. He found another rock and threw this one even harder. The splash was loud and angry.

"Oh, Burke," Dani sighed before she could stop herself. It was if he hadn't heard her because he kept right on talking.

"Finally, we ended up in a small place that wasn't much more than one room with a kitchenette and bathroom. She collected government welfare, and as long as I was quiet, didn't complain, and stayed out of her way, there was no trouble." Dropping her hand, he walked to the edge of the river. "I came home one day, and she was gone. She'd cleared out while I was at school. I found a new place to stay, got a job, and never looked back." He resumed his walk down the path, never once looking back to see if she followed him.

He had kept his explanation down to a bare minimum, and Dani knew this was probably the most he would ever say about his past. His childhood had been one of hunger and loneliness, and it was obvious that he had no idea what it was like to be part of a loving family. That much had become painfully clear to her from his seemingly endless fascination with her and her family. Christmas had shown her how much he had missed from his life, but knowing it herself, and actually hearing the stark details, were two different things. She ached for him, for all he had missed.

Burke was getting further away from her as he continued to stroll. Dani hurried down the path until she was walking alongside him again. "I'm sorry." It seemed like so little, but she really didn't know what else to say.

When he finally looked at her, his eyes were blazing with anger. "I don't want your damn pity!"

"That's not pity. It's compassion." She stopped him by simply placing her hand on his arm. "Your mother missed so much by not being involved in your life. In spite of all the obstacles, you've grown into a man any parent would be proud of."

"I'll never know that for sure, will I? If you spoke to anyone who worked with me they'd tell you I was a good businessman, ruthless and cold as hell. Not much else."

"Don't say that. I don't know what you were like before. I only know what you're like now. You're a bit arrogant at times, and you have very definite opinions, but I like you anyway." She gave Burke a teasing smile, hoping to lighten his mood.

"But you like me anyway, huh? It must be my good looks, if not my winning personality." A ghost of a smile flitted across his face as he lifted his hand and allowed his fingers to brush her cheek in a loving caress.

N. J. Walters

"You know I think you're very handsome," she answered tartly, moved by his gesture and desperate to keep from crying in front of him. "I just don't want it to go to your head. Besides," she added on a softer note, "there's no one else I'd rather be with than you. You've made my life so much richer just by being part of it."

He pulled her into his arms and held her tight, as if he couldn't bring himself to let her go. They stood like that for a long time, neither one of them wanting to let go. Both of them needing the contact with the other.

Burke pulled back first. His hands slowly moved up to frame her face, and he carefully bent forward and kissed first her forehead, then her cheeks, and finally her mouth. Soft kisses that spoke more than words. "Oh, Dani, what would my life be like without you? I don't want to go back to the way it was before."

"You don't have to. You're changing and growing, and that's not always easy. But sometimes it's necessary."

Burke stood and watched her for a moment as if digesting what she had said. Sighing deeply, he kissed the top of her head. As they resumed their walk, he tucked his hands back in his pockets, but this time one of hers was nestled in his coat pocket next to one of his.

"Tell me about your first job?"

It was the first specific question she had asked him and Burke laughed as he answered. "Nothing original I'm afraid. I got a job on a construction site doing grunt work."

"You obviously didn't do that forever. What did you do, start your own construction company, eventually?" Dani found

134

she was curious to know what kind of business Burke had owned. Up until now, he had been very vague about the whole thing, and she hadn't wanted to push. They walked in silence as she waited patiently for his answer.

Amazement filled him as he watched the woman walking by his side. For the first time in his life, he'd been able to talk about his past. It was if a huge burden had been lifted from his shoulders. She knew the worst, and she was still by his side. But old habits died hard, and Burke proceeded with caution. "You're partly right. I was a partner in a construction company that also had some real estate concerns."

What he didn't tell her was that the construction company was just one of many that his investment firm had a controlling interest in. Or that some of his real estate concerns had involved multimillion-dollar apartment complexes and shopping malls. In fact, Burke still owned some of those buildings. They were good investments.

He still didn't think Dani had any idea how much money he had. It was crazy, but he was afraid that if she knew he was rich, it would change the way she looked at him, and he was afraid to test their newfound happiness. It was such a reversal of the usual reasons he had for keeping his financial situation a secret that he smiled.

Dani squeezed his hand and smiled. "Real estate. I knew you were more than just a pretty face. So we have something else in common. We're both small business owners. I know my business is smaller than yours was, but the same principles apply."

"Yes, the same principles apply." A shiver racked her body, and he knew it was time to end their walk. "We better head back to the truck. You're getting cold."

As they turned and started walking back toward the warmth of the truck, he pulled Dani closer to his side to share his warmth, taking care to tuck her scarf more tightly around her neck. Their pace was brisk on their return trip.

"That's the past. What do you want to do with the future?"

"With the investments I've still got, I won't starve." Burke spoke slowly, trying to put into words some of the thoughts that he'd had. "I like what I do and business is what I know. I thought maybe I'd look around Jamesville and see if there are any investment possibilities." He shrugged, not quite sure what he was going to do yet. All he knew for certain was that he wanted to stay in Jamesville, close to her. "What do you think?"

Burke valued Dani's opinions. She had a good head on her shoulders and gave concise, well-thought-out advice when asked. It was one of the things he admired about her. His main concern now was how she felt about him staying in Jamesville and putting down roots there.

"That's an excellent idea. The town would certainly welcome any new investment, especially from someone with your business experience." She finished in a rush, obviously pleased with the idea.

He was taken aback by her quick and immediate support of his idea. She seemed to have no doubt that he could do this if he wanted to. Her faith in him pleased him immensely, because he knew she was sincere. She wanted him to succeed for himself, because it was what he wanted and not because she had anything to gain by it. Once again, he was the recipient of Dani's generosity, and it felt good. It also made him realize how selfish he was being, thinking only of himself.

"Dani, I know you've got your business, but that was something that came about by necessity. Was there anything you wanted to do when you were growing up?" He waited patiently while she gathered her thoughts.

"Well," Dani hesitated, but he nodded, silently encouraging her to continue. "Actually, I always thought I might write a book."

"Dani, that's wonderful. You're writing a book. How come you've never mentioned it before now?" His enthusiasm proved to be contagious, and she began to laugh. He was so proud of her, he had to stop and hug her. Picking her up in his arms, he swung her around in circles. Her laughter echoed through the night. Burke thought he'd never heard such a beautiful sound in his entire life.

When he finally put her down, it took a few minutes for her to catch her breath. "Actually, I'm not only writing a book, I already have five completed manuscripts. They're for children and all about the same adventurous young girl." She spoke quickly, as if all the words had been pent up inside her for so long that they came tumbling out at once. "I've never sent any of them to publishers, but I've already decided that this is the year I do it."

"Why haven't you done it already?" He was honestly amazed that someone would put so much effort into writing, not one, but five books, and not try to get them published.

"Not enough nerve, I guess." She shrugged as if it didn't matter. "Sending out manuscripts takes time and money, and for a few years, every extra penny counted. I always convinced myself the boys needed new clothes or the house need fixing, but really I think I was afraid of the rejection."

"I can understand that." He nodded at her, hoping to encourage her to keep talking.

"I researched publishers and agents at the library and put together packages to send out to a bunch of them." She laughed. "Now, I have all these envelopes, and I've been waiting for the courage to mail them."

"This really means a lot to you, doesn't it?" Burke was continually discovering that there was more to this complex woman than he'd even imagined. He'd had no idea that she'd had such plans or that she was close to putting them into action. But that was Dani. She just forged ahead, doing whatever she had to do, never complaining or, for that matter, bragging about it.

"Yes, it does. I know that publishing is a long shot." She gave him a self-effacing smile. "I won't quit the day job, but it's something I have to try."

"Do Patrick and Shamus know about your writing?" Burke asked Dani.

"Yes, they know. They took turns helping me learn how to use a computer so that it would be easier for me to write and edit my stories. Patrick saved money from his part-time job to help me buy us a computer for home, and Shamus was a big help with my research on publishers. He's a whiz on-line." Once again, her pride in her younger brothers shone through.

They reached the truck, and Burke opened the door, holding her hand and helping her climb up into her seat. He dropped a quick kiss on her palm before closing the door, going around to the driver's side, and climbing in beside her. He started the truck and turned on the heater. Dani began to shiver even harder, so he pulled her into his arms, offering her his body heat.

"I'm sorry. I shouldn't have kept you out in the cold for so long. I'd kiss you, but I'm afraid our lips would freeze together." He teased her as he ran his hands over her back and down her arms in an attempt to warm her.

"There's no where else I'd rather be. But I disagree with one thing you said."

Before he could ask what that was, Dani reached up and kissed him. Her soft lips brushed his, and he groaned in response. It was the first time she had kissed him since they had gotten back together. Sure, he had kissed her, as often as he could, but somehow it was important that she had initiated this herself. It made him feel as if he had somehow earned back some of her trust in him.

"If we don't stop, I might set the truck on fire," Burke's breathing was heavy and labored when he reluctantly pulled away.

"I know what you mean." Her soft smile warmed him. "Suddenly, I'm not cold anymore."

"I'm glad," Burke spoke simply. Pulling her into his side, he cuddled her close to him as he put the truck in drive and headed back to her house.

Chapter Twelve

Today couldn't get any worse. Since sleeping through her alarm and getting up a half-hour late, the day had steadily gone from bad to worse.

Dani had jumped into the shower first thing this morning, only to discover that all the hot water had been used up. Shivering, she had allowed the cold water to pound down on her head. On the bright side, at least it woke her up. Toweling off quickly, she hurried back to her room to dress.

Then her favorite sweater had started to unravel from the bottom. To top things off, when she finally dressed and raced downstairs to grab a cup of coffee before dashing off to her first cleaning job for the day, she knocked over her mug. Unable to pull back in time, she burned her hand, which was now blotchy red and stung. After running her hand under cold water to ease the pain, she had wasted even more time cleaning up the mess that had spilled all over the counter and the floor.

Pulling on her coat and boots, she raced to the truck, hoping to make up some time. She shoved the key into the ignition and turned. Nothing. She tried again. Nothing. Not a peep. Not a groan. Not a sputter. Nothing.

Sitting there in the cold truck with her head resting against the steering wheel, she wondered why she had even bothered to get out of bed where she'd been warm and toasty. Instead, she was cold, completely out of sorts, her hand ached, her head hurt, and she knew in her heart that her engine was dead.

"Why me?" Dani muttered the question aloud, not expecting an answer. It was a good thing, too, because she knew she wasn't going to get one. She had to write it off as cosmic bad luck. She just wished she had read her horoscope the night before. Maybe it would have warned her to stay in bed.

Slowly, she lifted her head. Ignoring the urge to beat it against the steering wheel a few times, she removed the key from the ignition. She opened the door and slammed it shut, just to make herself feel better. Still muttering to herself about the fates, she stomped to the back door of the house and let herself in.

Dani took off her coat, being careful not to bump her hand, which was now throbbing. She kicked off her boots, padded to the kitchen cupboards and took down a bottle of pain relievers. Shaking two out of the bottle, she chased them down with a glass of water. Taking a deep breath to calm herself, she pulled out a chair and sat at the kitchen table.

She made a mental list as she stared at the telephone. First, she had to cancel, and hopefully reschedule, all her work for today. Then she had to call Mike Sampson's garage and see if Mike could come out and look at the truck. She could only hope the problem was a cheap one. But with the way her luck was running today, she wasn't going to make any bets on it.

Dani started to reach for the phone but suddenly stopped. Decisively, she got up from the table, filled the kettle, and put it on the stove to boil. First things first, she needed chocolate. Rich, thick, steaming hot chocolate, loaded with marshmallows, to warm her up and give her the strength to face the rest of the day.

ॐ   ॐ   ॐ

"It's not good." Mike Sampson fiddled with some wires before finally looking up from under the hood of the truck. She sensed his reluctance to face her and knew that she wasn't going to like what he had to say.

"How bad?" Dani had known Mike all her life. His father had owned the garage in town for what seemed like forever, and he had taken it over last year when his father had semi-retired. Her father had done business with Mike's father for years. She trusted him to be honest and fair with her, and she knew by the look on his face that the news wasn't good.

"The engine is gone. From the look of things, it's a wonder that the thing didn't die sooner." Mike drew in a deep breath. "It's a write-off, Dani. The truck is fourteen years old. It'll cost you more to fix it than it is worth. I could put in a used engine, but you still need some brake work done, and the exhaust is nearly shot. You can get another opinion if you want, but the truck needs that much work and probably more. I wouldn't know for sure how much more until I took it into the shop."

She stared at him in shock. This was even worse than she had expected. Although she knew the truck had been operating on a wish and a prayer for the last year, she just never expected it to give out on her.

Mike slammed the hood of the truck, hauled a rag out of his back pocket, and wiped some of the grease and grime off his hands. "Listen, Dani. I can give you five hundred dollars for her for scrap. I also know that Jake Tanner is thinking about selling his old truck. It's only six years old, and it's in decent shape. I could call him and find out how much he wants for it."

Dani shook herself out of her daze. "I'd appreciate that, Mike. I don't know for sure what I'm gonna do yet, but I'd appreciate it if you'd speak to him for me." She didn't know Jake Tanner, except to see him.

"I've got to talk things over with the boys, but I'll get back to you on your offer." A decision this big couldn't be made quickly. She needed time to think. "Thanks for coming out so quickly this morning, even if it was a waste of your time. How much do I owe you for the trip?"

"Forget it. I didn't fix anything, so you don't owe me anything." Mike crossed his arms defiantly over his chest. "I'm not gonna add to your problem. Besides, my dad would have a fit if he heard." He offered her a boyish grin. "So you're really saving me from a calling down by the old man."

Dani laughed and shook her head. They both knew that her financial situation was tight at best. She knew he was trying to make this easy on her, which she really appreciated, but he had to make a living too. "I called you out here and I'll pay for your time." Her firm tone left no room for argument.

Mike thought for a minute, rubbing his hand through his hair in exasperation. He stopped suddenly. "I'll tell you what.

Since all you had was my time, how's about we trade for some of yours?"

Dani looked at him questioningly.

"Well, my in-laws are coming in two weeks, and Katie is busy with the new baby and all. Maybe you could come by and give her a half-hour of cleaning time. She'd really appreciate the help, and then she wouldn't work herself into a tizzy trying to get everything just so for her parents."

Satisfied, she held out her hand to seal the deal. "You've got a deal. I'll call Katie and tell her when to expect me for a morning's work." She shook his hand and spoke again before he could object. "You're doing me a favor by calling Jake Tanner about the truck, so I'll give Katie a morning of my time."

"All right then, you got yourself a deal. I'll call you as soon as I talk to Jake." Mike ambled back to his own truck, and giving her a final wave, he drove away.

        ð   *ð*   *ð*

Patrick knew something was wrong the minute he entered the kitchen. The smell of lemon polish filled the air. The house was always tidy, but this was different. This was super shiny, eat-off-the-floor clean. Besides, Dani should have been at work all day; she shouldn't have had time for housework.

"Dani, where are you?"

"Right here," Dani answered as she hurried down the hall toward him, dust cloth in hand. "How was work today?"

"Work was fine." He tugged open the refrigerator door and took out a bottle of juice. Tipping the bottle back, he took a mouthful. He pushed the door closed with his hip as he swallowed. "What happened today? Did one of your jobs get cancelled?"

"Oh, Patrick," Dani sighed. "I wish it was that simple. You better sit down."

Shamus came bounding through the front door at that moment. The sounds of his coat and boots coming off preceded him. "I'm home. What's for supper?" He was pulling off his sweater as he entered the kitchen. "I'm starving." Tossing the sweater on the back of a chair, he took one look at their faces and stopped in his tracks. "What's wrong?"

"You'd better sit down too." Dani pulled out a chair and sat, waiting until both he and Shamus were sitting before she spoke.

"The truck is dead."

"What do you mean, dead?" Patrick gripped the juice bottle tightly between his two hands.

"It wouldn't start this morning, and I had Mike come out from the garage. The engine is gone and various other parts are almost as bad. He said she's only fit for scrap."

Patrick whistled almost soundlessly and cut to the bottom line. "How much for scrap? And how much for another truck?"

"Five hundred for scrap and I've got a lead on a six-year-old truck."

"Whose truck?" Shamus plucked an apple out of the bowl on the table and crunched into it. Patrick shook his head, amazed at his brother. Nothing ever ruined Shamus' appetite.

"Mike said that Jake Tanner was selling his. He's going to call Jake and check on it for me. I'm hoping he'll call tonight, which is why we need to decide what to do. I can't go more than a few days without transportation." Dani rubbed at a nonexistent spot on the table, and Patrick knew she was fighting to keep her anxiety at bay. "I can't lose the money or the customers."

"Jake's truck is in good shape," Shamus spoke as he munched. "He comes in for gas now and then. I've filled the truck, and I can tell you the body is solid. I don't think Mike would recommend it if he hadn't figured the engine was sound."

"How are we going to finance it?" Patrick took another swig of juice while his mind worked on the problem.

"The only solution I've come up with, after thinking about it all day, is a bank loan." Dani shook her head. "There's no other way."

"We'll all help with the payments." Patrick's drained the bottle and clunked it on the table. "I can put in some overtime at work, no problem."

"Yeah, we'll both pitch in," Shamus seconded.

Dani shook her head before the words were out of their mouths. "I appreciate it, but you've both got to try and save money for school. I've got some in the bank for a down payment so the bank loan won't have to be for the total amount."

Patrick scowled as he sat forward in his chair and rested his arms on the table. "No way. You've worked too hard and too long to save that money. I'm working now, and I'll help pay."

"Patrick, I appreciate it, but I also know that you don't want to work as a landscaper your whole life. I know you're waiting until the spring to take the entrance exams to the police academy. You need that money for expenses and transportation of your own."

"I can put it off for another year." Patrick suddenly felt much older than his nineteen years. He might be her younger brother, but he was a man, and there was no way he would allow her to shoulder this burden alone. He'd just delay his future plans if he had to.

As if she'd read his thoughts, Dani scowled at him. "You will not put it off another minute longer than you have to. I need the truck, and I'll pay for the truck."

"What's going on?"

They all looked up as the new voice spoke. Burke lounged in the doorway, his shoulder propped against the doorframe and his arms folded across his chest. He looked like he had been standing there for a while.

"Burke, we didn't hear you come in," Dani smiled as she spoke.

"I knocked, but no one answered so I let myself in. Now what's going on here?"

"We're having a family conference." Shamus got up and dumped his apple core in the garbage. Taking his seat again, he reached out and plucked a banana out of the bowl.

"Do you want me to leave?" Burke shifted his stance in the doorway as if preparing to leave.

Patrick watched as his sister reached her hand out to Burke. The older man took it in his as he pulled out a chair.

"Oh no, Burke. Sit down." Dani tugged him down into the chair next to hers. "Maybe you can give us a fresh perspective on things."

Patrick smothered a chuckle in spite of his worries. His softhearted sister had obviously seen the hurt look in Burke's eyes and wanted to reassure him.

When Burke sat, he didn't relinquish his hold on her hand. "What's the problem?"

Before she could speak, the phone rang. "It's probably Mike. Please explain everything to Burke." She reached for the phone as she spoke, leaving him to explain everything. Patrick took a deep breath and leaned forward.

"Who's Mike?" Burke all but growled, surprised by the flash of jealousy that pierced him when Dani had mentioned another man's name so casually.

"Well," Patrick began, "it's like this..."

By the time Dani got off the phone with Mike, Patrick had finished telling him about the truck. Burke was a little stunned by it, although he knew he shouldn't be. He knew that the O'Rourke family didn't have much money, but this was another reminder of how tight things were for them. To him, this would be a minor inconvenience, but to them, it was a crisis.

They all looked at her as she sat down. "Mike says I can get it for five thousand. The truck is in great shape, and with what he'll give me for our truck, I'll have to come up with forty-five hundred. If I take off the money I've got saved, I'll only need a loan for two thousand."

"You can't use the money you've saved." Burke scowled at the thought. He knew that a loan would make her work even harder and that she would put off her plans for writing indefinitely. "You've got plans for that."

"Well, now I've got other plans for it. I don't have too much choice in the matter. I've got to have that truck." She tapped her fingers on the table as she thought.

"I'll loan you the money for the truck." Burke spoke calmly as he stared at Dani. Actually, the more he thought about it, the more he wanted to buy it for her.

"I can't let you do that." Dani sounded so shocked that Burke almost laughed. But his humor quickly died as she continued. "You can't tie up your money like that. You've got plans of your own. No, this is my problem, and I've figured out how I'm going to handle it." She nodded for emphasis as she spoke.

Patrick grabbed her hand to get her attention. "How about us? Shamus and I said we'll pay our share, and we will."

"No, Patrick. Both of you need your money for your schooling. I need the truck for my business, so I'll pay for it." Dani smiled at them to soften her words. "But thanks. Just knowing you want to help means a lot to me."

Burke could feel his anger rising at the casual way she had thrust aside his offer of help. Once again, he felt like an outsider, and he didn't like it one bit. He was a part of her life now, and the quicker she got used to that fact the better. "Don't be ridiculous, Dani. I said I'll loan you the money, and I will. If it makes you feel any better we can draw up an agreement between us and both sign it. You can pay me each month instead of the bank. And unlike the bank, I won't charge interest or come after you if you're late with a payment."

"Burke, I can't take your money." Dani looked puzzled at his vehemence.

149

"Why the hell not?" Burke roared as he stood, toppling his chair behind him. The crash of the chair on the floor was punctuated by a moment of stunned silence.

"Because it's yours, not mine. And the problem is mine, not yours." She stood slowly and faced him. His outburst had obviously surprised her. Well, she was in for a bigger surprise if she thought she could leave him out of her life and problems.

Toe to toe, they stood in the kitchen. Burke glared at her, and she glared right back. Patrick and Shamus had both surged to their feet at his unexpected outburst. They both stood, not saying a word, watching both Dani and Burke. It was obvious they were both ready to intervene if they thought it was necessary. That they thought he might hurt her drove Burke's temper even higher.

"Not my problem! Not my problem!" His fists were clenched at his sides to keep himself from grabbing her and shaking some sense into her. The woman infuriated him. "Listen sweetheart, I care a great deal about you, so it is my problem. You can't treat me like family for part of the time and like a stranger the rest. Not my problem! You're lucky I don't turn you over my knee and paddle you." Burke's voice got quieter as he finished, the anger reverberating in the low tone.

Dani stood still as a statue, stunned by his fury. He could see her mind mulling over what he'd said and reading between the lines. Suddenly, she lunged toward him, wrapping her arms around his neck and hugging him tight. Automatically, his arms went around her, and he held her as tight as he dared.

The woman had done it to him again. Just when he was mad as anything at her, she disarmed him completely by jumping into his arms. "I won't let you close me out," he muttered softly in her ear.

She tightened her hold on him, leaning close and whispering in his ear that she hadn't realized he would see her decision as closing him out. He knew she was so used to doing things on her own that she hadn't considered it from his point of view at all. He buried his face in her hair and swallowed back the lump in his throat.

Finally she broke away from his embrace. "All right. I'll take your offer of a loan. But only for the two thousand, and I will pay you interest, and we will have a written agreement."

Burke scowled. It wasn't exactly what he wanted, but at least she was letting him help her. "If that's the way you want it." Picking his chair up off the floor, he righted it before flopping back down onto it. "I still think you should let me loan you all of the money," he muttered. Not that he would ever take any money for the loan, but she didn't have to know that yet.

"Thank you, Burke." She wrapped her arms around him from behind and kissed his cheek. "It means a lot to me that you want to help me. But it also means a lot to me that you respect me enough to accept my opinion in this."

He could tell she was humoring him. Trying to calm the savage beast, as it were. And damned if it wasn't working. In spite of his attempt to hang onto it, his anger just seemed to empty out of him. He reached down and brought her hands to his lips and gently kissed them. Looking up, he stared at her, loving the soft twinkle in her eyes.

"Ahem," Patrick cleared his throat. "Remember us, your brothers, the other people who live in this house?" Both Patrick and Shamus had quietly retaken their seats when Burke had resumed his place at the table. Now they both sat with amused looks on their faces. Burke and Dani had put on quite a show.

Dani smiled sheepishly at her brother. "Sorry, I got sidetracked." She glanced up at Burke and gave him a smile in a way that told him he had the power to captivate her attention and that she had indeed forgotten about her brothers' presence. Burke found himself smiling back in return. He'd never admit that the same had happened to him.

Patrick knocked on the table to get their attention once again. "If you've settled this, then you'd better call Jake Tanner and make arrangements. Then we'll draw up an agreement and sign it." Patrick held out his hand to Burke as he spoke. "I'm going to sign it too, to guarantee Dani's side of the agreement. In the event something happens and she can't make a payment, I'll pay."

"That will be just fine," Burke shook Patrick's hand to seal the agreement. This family had a lot of pride, and he understood that sometimes pride was all you had, and it was important. "You better call that Tanner fellow, Dani, and tell him we can come out tomorrow and look at the truck, if it's convenient."

Dani looked from one man to another as Shamus just sat there with his chair tipped back on two legs and grinned at them as if they were all mad. She pushed his chair forward so that all four legs were firmly on the floor. When he gave her a sheepish grin, she reached out and tousled his hair. He swatted at her playfully as she pulled away.

As she reached for the phone, she gave Patrick a peck on the cheek, just to say thank you. He didn't turn away, but his cheeks turned pink.

She patted Burke's arms as she placed her call, just wanting to touch him.

She knew that both Patrick and Burke had given in as much as they were going to. She had to remember that they had as much pride as she did, probably more, being men.

Dani felt good about the arrangement. She would pay back every penny to Burke, but she felt that the whole thing had brought them closer. The fact that he was willing to loan her the money was also a good sign that he might be settling down here in Jamesville. After all, you didn't loan someone that much money and then just forget about it.

Her thoughts were interrupted when a male voice answered the phone. "Good evening, Mr. Tanner. This is Dani O'Rourke calling. I hear you have a truck for sale…"

Chapter Thirteen

Dani shook hands with the green-eyed, solidly built man in front of her, a huge grin on her face. "You've got yourself a deal, Mr. Tanner."

"Please, call me Jake." Jake seemed pleased that his truck had sold so quickly and for the price he had asked. "Come on in the house, and we'll get all the papers signed over and a bill of sale made out."

Burke, who had hovered in the background during the discussion, took her hand as they walked toward the two-story white farmhouse. It had taken all of his willpower not to take over and handle the sale himself. He had restrained his natural inclination only because he knew it was important to Dani to handle this herself. But he had checked out the truck and was satisfied that it was in good working order.

He felt Tanner was trustworthy, but he would take no chances. He planned to make sure all the paperwork was in order before Dani gave Jake the certified check she had brought with her. It still galled him that she would only let him loan her part of the money. Heck, he wanted to buy her a new truck. The cost of one wasn't much to him, but he knew she still had no idea of his financial worth.

That was something he was going to have to tell her soon. It didn't worry him too much. After all, she knew he'd had a successful business; she just didn't know *how* successful.

She gave his hand a squeeze as they followed Jake through the backdoor and into the kitchen, at the back of the house. It didn't take long to finalize the transaction. Burke scrutinized the papers over Dani's shoulder as she took her time examining them. Jake had provided a bill-of-sale, receipts for some recent work he'd had done on the vehicle, and all the necessary ownership papers. Everything seemed to be in order. Dani gave Jake her check, and he gave her the keys. Both parties were pleased as they shook hands to finalize the deal. Jake had his money, and she had her new truck.

She practically danced down the driveway as she hurried toward her new vehicle. "Thank you for coming out with me, Burke, and for letting me handle things with Jake. You actually behaved yourself quite well." Her teasing grin told him just how pleased she was. "I know it was hard for you not to jump in and take over."

"You mean you can dress me up and take me places?" Burke tapped a finger on the tip of her nose. "You look pleased with yourself. I can assume, then, that you're happy with your new truck." He found her happiness infectious.

"Isn't it wonderful, Burke? It's almost like new, it's in such good shape. Green's my color, don't you think?" Lovingly, she stroked her hand over the hood of the truck, frowning when her hand came back dusty. "It'll look even better as soon as I polish it up a bit."

"Yeah, I think green is your color." Leaning over, he gently kissed the frown from her lips.

Dani sighed and leaned into his kiss. Her arms slowly crept up over his chest and around his neck as she held him tight. Pulling her closer, he deepened the kiss. He was starved for her taste. Nothing in the world tasted as good as Dani's lips. He never wanted to let go.

The sound of voices brought Burke back to reality with a thud. She had done it to him again. Somehow when he kissed her, he had a tendency to forget where he was. And where he was right now was the middle of Jake Tanner's driveway.

He carefully pulled Dani's arms from around his neck. "We'll finish this later, honey," Burke promised.

"Promises, promises." Dani taunted as him as she climbed aboard the truck and settled herself behind the wheel. She put the key in the ignition, turned it, and the truck roared to life.

She took a moment to familiarize herself with the interior. Turning the lights on and off, cleaning her windshield, she checked out her new acquisition. Burke thought she was just like a kid with a new toy. Her joy was a wonderful thing to share.

Leaning against the open door, he laughed as he watched her. "I've got to take care of some things, but I'll see you later tonight. Drive carefully. You wouldn't want to scratch your new truck." Bending down, he planted a quick kiss on her lips, closed the driver's door, and headed for his own vehicle.

Dani turned the radio up on bust and pulled the truck out of the driveway. She blew her horn and waved to him as she passed him. He knew she had two jobs this afternoon, and then she had to grocery shop. He put his truck in gear and pulled out behind her, already looking forward to seeing her again later tonight.

≈ ≈ ≈

As Dani loaded grocery bags into the front seat of her truck, she reflected on the changes she and Burke had gone through since Christmas. Today had marked a new phase in their relationship. They were building a relationship that was based on mutual respect, honesty, trust, and caring.

She held a hope in her heart that Burke was coming to care deeply for her. She was almost afraid to even think of marriage, but deep in her soul she knew that was what she wanted. She wanted to marry Burke and build a life with him here in Jamesville. She wanted them to buy an old farmhouse and make it a home together, complete with children and a dog. She would write and run her cleaning business and Burke would...well, Burke would do whatever he decided to do.

So wrapped up in her own thoughts, it took Dani a moment to realize that she was no longer alone. She glanced up and was immediately wary when she saw the blonde woman leaning against the front of her truck.

Cynthia reached out and ran her index finger over the hood of the truck. She took her time drawing a large heart in the dust. "Well, well, you've come up in the world a little these days, haven't you? But a used truck! I would have thought you could have gotten your lover to buy you a new one. Maybe you're not that good, after all." Cynthia looked Dani up and down as she spoke. "Your hair is not bad, but your figure is less than fashionable. Your taste in clothes runs more to boys' hand-me-downs than to anything attractive. Perhaps you're worth a used truck."

Stunned by the vicious attack, Dani just stood there for a moment unable to comprehend the other woman's contempt. Her own rising anger came to her rescue, and when she spoke, it was with barely restrained fury. She had a very vivid memory of her last conversation with Cynthia.

"I bought this truck myself. As for my relationship with Burke, it's none of your business." Dani slammed the passenger door shut and just glared at the other woman.

"Little Miss Innocent, aren't you," Cynthia mocked. "I know for a fact that Burke took several thousand dollars out of the bank. Then, presto, you have a truck."

Dani's face paled, and her mouth dropped open. She was shocked by Cynthia's knowledge of Burke's finances, and in her anger, she spoke hastily. "Not that it's any of your business, but it's a private loan."

Dani groaned inwardly even as the words left her mouth. She didn't know why she allowed Cynthia to goad her into defending herself. Because Cynthia's father was the bank president, Dani knew that the other woman would have no problem getting information that she shouldn't have access to. In fact, Dani had seen several of the male employee's at the bank vie for Cynthia's attention. Any one of them would give her the information she wanted if she flattered them and flirted with them.

"I'll bet. What did you put up for collateral?" The look she gave Dani was intended to leave no room for doubt. "If I were you, I would have gotten a new truck, and I wouldn't even have had to sleep with him to do it. But then you don't have as much to offer as I do."

Dani's whole body was rigid. Her fists were clenched at her sides, and she knew she had to get away before she was tempted to use them on the other woman. Dani ignored Cynthia as she stalked around the back of the truck to the driver's side, not wanting to pass in front of Cynthia, who was leaning casually on the hood. All Dani wanted to do was to get in and drive away.

Realizing she was about to lose her audience, Cynthia straightened up and casually flicked her artfully styled hair over her shoulder. Smiling, she let loose with her final piece of malicious gossip. "Well, I suppose you can understand why a man like Burke would play games with you. He's just slumming for fun. When he's ready, he'll come back to his own kind of people and back to me." She laughed and played with a long gold chain that hung around her neck, running it back and forth between her fingers as Dani came to an abrupt halt.

Dani said nothing. She waited like a cornered animal, knowing instinctively that Cynthia was coming in for the final kill. Dani wanted to run, but she was rooted to the ground, waiting for whatever blow the other woman was ready to send her way.

"After all," Cynthia gloated. "A man as rich as Burke Black will naturally be drawn back to people in his own class as soon as he's fully recovered from his accident."

"What do you mean, rich?" Dani asked, unable to stop herself.

"Why, he's worth millions. Why, surely *you* knew." The sultry blonde sauntered over to where Dani was clutching the door handle. "I didn't know, but Daddy recognized his name immediately. Daddy's been away a lot on business since Christmas, so he didn't even know Burke was here until I mentioned it to him. Daddy says it's obvious that he doesn't want anyone here to know that he's an international business tycoon. That way he can indulge in a little cheap R&R." Cynthia patted Dani's arm sympathetically.

"I understand now why he only took me out once," Cynthia continued in a condescending tone. "He didn't want to link his name to mine until he was ready to return to business and his real life. When he does, he'll need a woman in his own class. He knows that I won't mind his little indiscretion with you. After all, it doesn't really mean anything to him." She gave Dani's arm a final pat. "You understand how these things are, don't you? Men can be pigs sometimes, but when they're that rich, you just have to forgive them."

Hooking her purse over her shoulder, she gave Dani a parting smile. "Well, I really must be going. I have to buy a new dress. Daddy says we'll throw a party for Burke when he's ready, and I'll need something new to wear." With that she turned and sauntered off, a spiteful smile on her face.

Dani gripped the door handle so tight her hand was white. She didn't know how long she stood there until a horn sounded next to her. She automatically waved at Jessie as she drove by. Forcing herself to open the door, Dani climbed inside the truck.

She took a deep breath and then another. Then denial rose up in her. Cynthia had to be lying. It certainly wouldn't be the first time. All Dani had to do was find Burke. There had to be some explanation. Cynthia was lying. She had to find Burke.

She repeated those two things over and over as she carefully drove home. Slowly, she unloaded the groceries into the house and put them all away. She made herself a cup of tea and sat at the kitchen table to wait. There had to be an explanation. All she had to do was wait.

&ve;&ve;&ve;

Burke felt better than he had in a long time. His leg was getting stronger and he was more relaxed than he'd been in years. He found himself humming one of Dani's favorite country songs as he opened the back door to her house. He didn't even bother to knock anymore. He felt like he belonged here.

"Dani, where are you, honey?" Burke called.

"Right here." Dani stood motionless in the kitchen door.

Burke heard the flat, lifeless tone of her voice and knew that something was wrong. He quickly crossed the kitchen and took her in his arms.

"What's wrong? Are you all right? Are the boys okay?" It took her a moment to answer, and Burke found the muscles in his body tensing, preparing for action, the longer it took.

"I'm really not sure if I'm okay or not. I had an unexpected chat with someone today and I was told some things that upset me." Her eyes begged him for reassurance.

"Tell me who it was."

"Cynthia James."

Disgust filled him at the mention of the other woman. "What did she want?"

Dani watched him carefully as if she was looking for some kind of response from him. It was hard, but he waited patiently for Dani's reply, holding her gently in his arms, silently encouraging her to confide in him.

"She had some story about you being a millionaire, and that you were just slumming with me and my family while you recovered from your accident, and that when you were ready to return to your life, you'd just dump me and leave." She said it all in one breath, as if afraid she would lose her nerve if she stopped for even a second.

Burke was aware the Dani had gone very still in his arms. He could hear the fear in her voice as she spoke.

"Tell me she lied, Burke. Please."

He knew that the time had come to tell Dani the truth. He would have preferred to do it in his own time, but he no longer had that luxury.

"Dani, I care for you very much. You know that." He rubbed his hands up and down her back as he spoke, wanting to reassure her that everything would be okay. "I am trying to build a new life, and I have no intention of going back to my old one."

"But?" He could see the apprehension in her eyes before she glanced away.

"But I really do have a great deal of money. But that doesn't make any difference to us and how we feel about each other." He watched her carefully, uncertain as to how she would react.

When she wouldn't look at him, Burke took her chin in his hand and tilted it slightly upward until she looked at him. He locked his eyes on hers, willing her to believe him. "It doesn't make any difference to us."

Shock was plain on her face as she held onto the one fact that seemed to bother her the most. "You lied to me."

"No," Burke countered. "You knew that I'd had a successful business. You just didn't know how profitable. Why does it matter? We're still the same people."

"Why did you lie to me?" He could see the hurt look in her eyes as she continued. "Did you think I was some little gold-digger after your money?"

Burke pulled away and stared at her, the disbelief plain in his eyes. "You don't really believe that, do you?"

"I don't know what to believe. It seems as if Cynthia knows things about you that I don't." She blinked hard, obviously trying to fight back the tears that welled up in her eyes. "What else don't I know, Burke?"

"You know everything important about me. I don't see what difference my bank balance makes." All he wanted to do was dry Dani's tears, but he forced himself to release her and take a step back. His growing anger warred with his need to comfort her. "Maybe it's me who doesn't really know you."

"What do you mean by that?" Dani snapped back. "You're the one who lied to me."

"Just what I said," Burke replied. He felt his anger and disappointment disappear behind a layer of calm control. He couldn't believe that Dani would think the worst of him after all they had been through together. Opening himself up emotionally to another person had been a mistake. One it was time to fix.

"Obviously, how much money I have makes a difference to you. If I were poor, we wouldn't be having this conversation. You're afraid of the fact I have money." Burke was warmed up now and all his bitter resentment spilled out as he just kept on going. "I thought we were building a relationship, but you're willing to believe the worst of me out of the mouth of a woman who is nothing but a troublemaker. You'd believe her over me."

"But you lied to me," Dani stood with her arms crossed defensively across her chest.

Burke rubbed the back of his neck and sighed. "No," he replied wearily, "I just didn't give you the bottom line of my bank account. I'm tired of trying to prove myself to you, Dani. What it comes down to is you still don't trust me, and I don't know what else I can do to make you believe in me."

"I did trust you, but you hid part of yourself from me." She trembled visibly now. "I don't know what to do."

Part of Burke wanted to take Dani in his arms and comfort her, and the other part of him just wanted to leave, to protect himself from further hurt. "And that's the problem. You have to decide if you trust me or not, because I'm through trying to prove myself. I don't want a woman who doesn't trust me. One who'll believe the worst about me." His voice was much calmer than he felt. "No, Dani, I don't want that at all."

"You don't make it easy." She looked more confused than ever. "You say that the money doesn't change our relationship, but it evidently meant enough to you to hide it from me. You say this is about trust, but you didn't trust me not to want your money more than you."

Her statement hit him hard, because he knew it held an element of truth. He ignored that little voice that said she might have a point and went on the offensive. "You have to decide, Dani. You either trust me or you don't. And while you're deciding that, I have to decide if I want to be with a woman who would be so quick to condemn me and believe the worst about me. If you were looking for an excuse to end our relationship, then you've just found it."

"I'll be around for a while. You know where to find me." Burke turned away and then stopped and fished a piece of paper out of his pocket. "Here's the note for your loan. Consider it paid as a parting gift."

Carefully, he laid the piece of paper on the counter and quietly let himself out the back door. He no longer felt as if he belonged there. Maybe it had always been an illusion.

Dani stood there staring at the closed door. What had just happened? Both of them had professed the need to have the other trust them, but neither one had been willing to trust. She had every right to be mad at Burke for finding out about his financial situation from Cynthia. But, on the other hand, he hadn't really lied; it had been more of an omission. But she felt that he did, however, owe her some explanation as to his actions.

Had she accused him of thinking she was a gold-digger because deep down she still didn't trust him not to hurt her? Was this her way of hurting him? She just didn't know. She did know that she shouldn't have let him go. They needed to talk things out calmly, not fight. Dani raced to the front door to stop Burke, but she was too late. She watched the truck turn the corner at the end of the street, unable to stop it.

Chapter Fourteen

Burke slammed the front door of the cabin behind him. His movements jerky, he pulled off his coat and boats and stomped toward the kitchen. How dare Dani accuse him of lying to her! Yanking open the refrigerator door, he grabbed a beer, popped the top, and took a swallow. He swiped at his mouth as he stalked back to the living room. Slumping on the sofa, he took another pull on the beer bottle before he laid it on the coffee table in front of him.

The anger that had filled him slowly seeped away as the ramifications of their fight hit him. Were he and Dani finished? He should never have left. He had allowed his own anger to make him act before he thought. But what else was he supposed to do? Dani had hurt him more than he thought he could ever be hurt. He had thought that his money wouldn't matter, but it had. Just not in the way he had assumed it would.

Burke wallowed for five whole minutes on the sofa before he got up and went over to the dining table where he had his laptop computer set up. He turned on the machine and pulled up a chair in front of it. There was nothing he could do until Dani had a chance to calm down. They both needed time to think. In the meantime, he would do what he always did when life had disappointed him. He would work. If he worked long enough and hard enough, maybe then some of the pain would go away.

The pounding on his door roused Burke from in front of his computer. He had no idea what time it was, but it was dark outside. Automatically, he saved what he was working on. Someone pounded on the door again. His heart leapt as his head cleared. Maybe it was Dani. He hurried across the room and flung the door open. His heart sank.

"Come on in, Patrick." Stepping back, he motioned the other man inside.

Patrick slowly entered the cabin. His hands were jammed in his coat pockets, and Burke appreciated the fact that the younger man kept them there, even though the scowl on his face made it obvious that Patrick was very angry.

"I'm trying to keep an open mind about this, but Dani is obviously very upset about something, and she's not talking to me. You know anything about that?"

Burke sighed, knowing he had to deal with Patrick when he'd rather just lose himself in his work. "Sit down, and I'll get us something to drink."

Burke went to the kitchen, rummaged through the refrigerator, and grabbed a couple of sodas before going back into the living room. Although he felt like he could use another beer, it was probably better for both of them that he keep his wits about him.

Patrick had removed his jacket and slung it across the back of the sofa, but he hadn't sat down. Instead he paced back and forth across the short length of the room. Burke noted that Patrick's hands were fisted and swung by his sides as he paced.

The younger man glared at Burke as he laid one of the sodas on the table. Burke ignored him and took his time opening the can of drink and settling himself into the comfortable rocking chair.

"Will you tell me what's going on?" Patrick demanded. He stopped pacing and faced Burke. His whole body was rigid with anger.

"I have money." Burke watched Patrick, waiting for his response.

"So?" His hands reached out and gripped the back of the sofa as he leaned closer to Burke.

"So, that's what Dani is upset about."

"There has to be more to it than that."

"That's the bottom line. I have money, Dani accused me of thinking she's a gold-digger, and now she doesn't trust me." Burke closed his eyes for a moment and leaned back in the chair. It hurt just to think about it all over again. He opened his tired eyes and took pity on the younger man. "Sit down, Patrick."

Patrick looked totally confused as he slowly took a seat. "Let me get this straight. Dani's mad because she found out you have money. Why didn't you just tell her yourself?"

"At first, I was afraid to tell her because a lot of women like me for that very reason. After I got to know Dani, I knew that it wouldn't matter to her." Burke's laugh was without humor. "At least I thought it wouldn't matter."

"So how did she find out?" Patrick finally picked up the soda from the table and took a drink.

"Cynthia James apparently found out and told Dani."

"Oh geez, Burke. Another woman told her." Sitting forward, he shook his head in disgust. "That's the worst way she could have found out."

Patrick was silent for a few moments, and Burke said nothing, giving the younger man the time he needed to pull his thoughts together.

"You see, Dani is insecure when it comes to relationships. She can do anything in business with confidence, but she never dated before you, and this thing today shook her confidence. If she means anything to you, give her some time." Patrick reached over and grasped Burke's arm. "She'll think about it and come around. She loves you, and that's why this hurt her so much."

"She loves me," Burke repeated, not quite willing to believe.

"Of course she does. What's wrong with the two of you?" Slumping back in his seat, he rolled his eyes skyward as if seeking assistance from a greater power. "You're supposed to be the adults. Open your eyes, for heaven's sake."

Burke looked at Patrick and shook his head. "Someday I'll remind you of this conversation when you're on my end."

Patrick's hearty laughter filled the room. "I'm sure you will."

Burke sat quietly in the rocker, pondering the situation. Patrick waited patiently and sipped his soda, absently tapping the can with his fingers.

Reaching a decision, he surged to his feet. "I'm going away for a few days. No, a week." He paced to the table and pulled his schedule up onto the screen. "I should be able to get things done in a week."

"You're coming back, right?" Patrick questioned.

Burke rounded quickly. "Of course, I'm coming back." Seeing the question in the younger man's eyes, Burke did something he rarely did. He explained himself. "Dani means more to me than she knows. I have to come back."

"What are you going to do?" Patrick came to his feet and eyed Burke cautiously.

"Just wait and see, just wait and see." He headed to the bedroom to pack. "Let yourself out, will you, and I'll see you in a week."

"I hope you know what you're doing, Burke," Patrick muttered as pulled on his coat and let himself out the front door.

&ep;   &ep;   &ep;

Dani lay in bed and watched the sun peek over the horizon. She hadn't slept at all last night. Her mind just kept going around in circles, replaying the conversations she'd had with both Cynthia and Burke.

Dani knew that it was the fact that Cynthia was privy to important information about Burke that she wasn't that had angered her the most. Her pride had been hurt. There, she admitted it to herself. Her pride had been hurt, and she'd lashed out at Burke.

She couldn't get him out of her mind. The look of hurt and disappointment on his face when she had confronted him haunted her. Until that very moment, she hadn't realized that she had the power to hurt him as much as he had to hurt her.

Pushing aside the comforter, she padded over to stand in front of the window. Easing the curtains aside, she stared at the melting snow and made a decision. Either she trusted Burke or she didn't. Either she loved him enough to work this out or she put him out of her life forever.

Filled with purpose, she walked over to her dresser and looked at herself in the mirror. She saw the same face that she saw every morning. It wasn't a beautiful face, yet Burke had called her beautiful. But more than that, he made her feel beautiful. Deep in her heart, she knew that Burke was an honest man.

Squaring her shoulders, she looked straight at the woman staring back at her. "If you love him, you'll go to him and work things out. Now. Right now, before you hurt each other more than you already have."

Decision made, she grabbed a quick shower before pulling on her clothes and heading for the door. She snagged her coat and keys on the way out. So what if the sun was barely up? This was too important to wait.

Dani was a woman on a mission. That mission was love. Anyone who had ever said that love was easy had obviously never been in love. Being in love was hard work. There were no easy answers or a straight path. The road to happiness was twisted and littered with debris, but she hoped that it was worth the effort. Nothing worthwhile ever came easy, so why should love be any different?

Easing the truck to a stop in front of Burke's cabin, she jumped out and raced to the front door. She pounded on the front door before she gave herself time to think. She would tell him immediately that she loved him and trusted him.

She waited expectantly. And waited. She bounced up and down to keep warm in the early morning cold.

He must be a sound sleeper, she thought as she pounded on the door again.

"Burke, open up, it's Dani," she called when the pounding received no answer. She cupped her hands over her eyes and peered through the small glass in the door, but could see nothing but the empty living room.

Dani got a sinking feeling in the pit of her stomach. She turned and scanned the driveway. Burke's truck was gone.

"No, don't panic. He probably couldn't sleep either," she muttered as she dragged herself back to her truck. He was probably just gone out for a drive or maybe an early breakfast. As disappointed as she was, she knew she would see him later. It was probably just as well. She must look like a wild woman after tearing out of bed and over here in such a hurry. Come to think of it, she hadn't even brushed her hair after she'd dried it, just slammed down the hair dryer and ran. Her hand went to her head, and she tucked her hair behind her ears.

Dani decided that she would go to work early since she was already up. The only thing on her schedule today was a house that had to be cleaned before the new owners moved in, and she had picked up the key yesterday. That way she could get home early and plan a special supper for her and Burke. But first, she would swing by the house and grab a cup of coffee and pick up her work supplies.

∾   ∾   ∾

The phone was ringing when she rushed through the back door later that afternoon. She dumped her purse on the counter and grabbed it quickly, hoping it was Burke. "Hello," she gasped, nearly out of breath.

"Dani?"

"Yes, this is Dani," she answered, trying to hide her disappointment.

"This is Silas Carter."

"Hello, Mr. Carter. What can I do for you?" Crossing her fingers, she hoped he had another job for her and hadn't called to cancel an existing one. She needed to start replacing the money she had spent on the truck.

"I've got a job for you if you've got the time. It's out at the Cozy Cabins," Silas answered.

"Of course I've got time. What unit and when?" Digging out her appointment book from her purse, she opened it.

"Unit number five, the one Mr. Black was in."

"What did you say?" It was a wonder he could hear her hoarse whisper.

"Unit five. Mr. Black dropped off his key last night before he left town. As soon as you can fit it in, Dani, if that's no problem."

"No, no problem," Dani heard herself answer.

"Good. I'll see you when you pick up the key."

Dani heard the click as Mr. Carter disconnected, and she slowly lowered the phone back to its cradle. This couldn't be happening. Burke had decided that he didn't want a woman who didn't trust him. She had driven him away. Or, that little voice in the back of her head taunted, had he been that serious about her after all?

Dani didn't know what to do. She realized suddenly that she had no notion of where to find Burke. She didn't know where he might have gone. If he didn't call her, she would never know.

"No, no, no," Dani wailed. "It's not supposed to happen this way."

"Dani, what's wrong?" She turned to find Patrick standing in the doorway, drawn to the kitchen by the sound of her voice.

"He's gone. He's gone, and I don't know where to find him." Grabbing her brother by his upper arms, she shook him. "I don't know where to find him."

"Who? Burke?" Patrick reached out and took Dani's hands from his arms and held them tight in his.

"Yes, he's gone," she said in a tortured whisper.

"Dani, it's okay. It's okay." Patrick put his arms around her, hugging her tight. "He's coming back."

Dani pulled back in surprise. "How do you know he's coming back?" Her voice went from pitiful to sharp in a flash.

"I went to see him yesterday," Patrick answered cautiously.

"You went to see him?"

"Well, yeah. I knew something had happened. Anyway, while I was there Burke said he had to go away for a week, but that he'd be back."

"Where is he?" Dani asked hopefully.

"I don't know," Patrick answered her. "All I know is that he said he'd be gone about a week, and then he'd be back."

"You're sure he said he was coming back?" Dani begged for reassurance.

"Yes, he'll be back. I think he needs to think about some things. You really hurt him, Dani."

"I know. We both hurt each other. We didn't mean to, but we did. I guess I'll just have to wait until he comes back to talk to him."

"Don't worry, Dani, everything will be okay." He tucked a stray lock of hair behind her ear. "I don't think you'll get rid of him too easily."

"I hope you're right, Patrick."

Needing time to think, she headed upstairs to her room. She had to be ready if Burke came back. No, *when* he came back. And he would be back, she reassured herself. They needed to really talk about what had happened. She was ready now to listen to what he had to say, ready to offer him reassurance that his money didn't matter to her. And then she had to apologize, because she knew she had hurt him deeply. She had to make him understand that they had a future together and that she loved him.

And she would, just as soon as he returned.

Chapter Fifteen

Over and over, she reassured herself that Burke was coming back. As the next seven days passed, she wavered back and forth between anger and tears. One minute, she just wished he were here so she could hold him, and the next minute, she wanted him here so she could yell at him for putting her through such agony.

Sleep came less and less, and her appetite dwindled. The longer he was gone, the harder it was for her to hold onto hope. She began to wonder if she would ever see him again.

She knew she was worrying both Patrick and Shamus, but she couldn't seem to help herself. The only thing that helped was work. The harder she worked, the less time she had to think. And the less she had time to think, the less she worried.

On the bright side, she had not only lost the three pounds she gained Christmas, but two more as well. Some women ate during times of stress, but she cleaned. Not only had she made more money by taking on extra jobs, but their own house had never been cleaner. She'd even cleaned out the linen closet. If Burke didn't show up soon, she'd be forced to mess things up just so she'd have something to clean. It was pathetic.

By the morning of the eighth day, she began to sense that even Patrick was no longer certain about Burke's return. Her brother became quiet and moody, watching her constantly, as if waiting for her to dissolve into tears.

Dani refused to give in to her feeling of despair.

She was convinced that Burke was gone for good. She was too sad to be angry. The whole world appeared as if it were a black and white movie. All the color was gone. Life was something to be gotten through one moment at a time, and food was something to be eaten to keep up her strength. If she had been the heroine of a Victorian Romance, she might have taken to her bed in decline. But she was a modern businesswoman with obligations who knew she would survive no matter what. Experience had taught her that life goes on and this too would pass, no matter how painful it was now.

It was for this very reason that she took another cleaning job from Silas Carter. He had sold the old Baker farmhouse and the surrounding ten acres it was on. Dani had always loved the charming home and it was for this reason, and to keep herself extra busy, that she took the job even though she was already booked solid.

The new owner wanted to move in immediately, Mr. Carter had informed her. So here she was at seven-thirty Saturday morning dragging her cleaning supplies into the Baker farmhouse. It was this very house that had inspired the setting for her children's books.

That reminded her of her promise to herself to mail out her manuscripts to perspective agents and publishers. She made a promise to herself right then and there that she would mail her first submission before the end of the week.

Leaving her belongings on the kitchen counter, she wandered around the empty house. The kitchen was big and quite charming, almost a larger version of her own. She ran her hand lovingly across the kitchen counter, wondering if the new owners had a large enough family to fill such a wonderful kitchen.

She meandered slowly through the house, admiring the living room and falling in love with the library that had an alcove that was almost like an indoor green house. With glass on three sides, it would be like sitting outside, even in the middle of winter. Climbing up the pine staircase to the bedroom area, she peeked in all the rooms and finally found herself standing in the middle of what was certainly the master bedroom.

It was a large room with two tall windows, from floor to ceiling, that invited in the morning sunshine. There were two spacious closets, his and hers. Dani closed her eyes and imagined a brass bed with a meadow green comforter. She would have several rugs in shades of green and sunshine yellow curtains. There was also room for two wicker chairs with cushions in yellow and green. Put a small table between them and they would make a lovely sitting area next to one of the windows.

Sighing, she slowly opened her eyes. What must it be like to own such a place? To be planning a future and a life with the person you love. Dani shook herself to dispel her daydreams. She had to stop thinking like this or she would start crying again.

N. J. Walters

"What do you think you're doing?" The soft male voice queried from the open doorway.

Dani had been asked much that same question before, but this time the voice was not angry. Slowly, she turned to the doorway.

"Burke," Dani found she could barely speak his name. "What are you doing here?" Shock held her rooted in place as her hand went to her mouth. She hadn't heard a sound. It appeared she had conjured him from her thoughts.

Burke walked slowly toward her. His eyes never left her face as he reached out and wrapped his arms around her. "Oh no, you don't, sweetheart. If you're going to break and enter, you have to take the consequences."

She didn't know whether the laugh, cry, or scream. "I'm not here to break and enter. I'm here to clean."

His laughter washed over her as he rocked her back and forth in his embrace. "It seems to me I remember us playing out this particular scene before."

"What are you doing here, Burke?" Dani asked softly. Her hands pushed against his chest, and he automatically loosened his hold on her.

All laughter fled from his face. His hands covered hers, as if he could not bear to lose contact with her. "I'm here to be with you."

"How long this time before you leave without a word?" Despite her desire to hold onto him forever, she forced herself to pull away from him. He reluctantly released her hands and stepped back. A scowl now covered his face, making the scar on his cheek even more prominent. She longed to soothe the anger from him, but held her ground.

"What do you mean?" Crossing his arms over his chest, he waited.

"I didn't know if you were ever coming back. I didn't know if you had decided you didn't want a woman who wouldn't trust you or if what Cynthia had told me was true." It hurt her to speak these things out loud, but she knew that they had to clear up all their misunderstandings if they were to go forward from here.

"Didn't Patrick tell you I was coming back?" Burke's face turned thunderous, and his voice grew louder with every word he spoke.

"Yes, he did. But, you've been gone eight days without a word, and we didn't part under the best of circumstances." Remembered pain brought tears to Dani's eyes. She blinked hard to ward them off. "You know, I went out to the cabin early the next morning to talk to you, but you weren't there. I thought that you were just out early, like I was, until Mr. Carter called me to clean your cabin."

"Oh, Dani," Burke whispered as he tried to pull her back into his comforting embrace.

She stepped away, knowing she had to finish this and that she lost the ability to think coherently when Burke held her in his arms. "Patrick told me you were gone. I got mad first, because I'm honestly tired of finding out important things like this from other people." She tapped a finger on his chest for emphasis. "Then I was sad and hurt. Finally, I was afraid that you might not come back."

"I thought that you needed the time to think things over." Burke had a slightly bewildered look on his face. "It didn't occur to me that you would think that I wouldn't come back." Reaching out once again, he wrapped an arm around her waist and dragged her close. This time she allowed him to pull her close.

"I've got to know, Burke. Where do we stand? I've been afraid to ask, but I find now that I'm more afraid not to ask." She stared deep into his eyes, hoping to see the answer there. "Are you staying here in Jamesville? Do we have a future?"

His body was very still, and for a moment, he said nothing. Suddenly, he took a deep breath and exhaled slowly. "Dani, honey." Burke's large hands reached up and caressed her face. "Haven't you figured it out yet? This is my house."

Now she was totally confused. "Your house. When did you buy it?"

"That's why I've been gone this last week. I'm going to be running my business concerns from here. I've had people out here all week connecting the electricity and phone lines for my office that I'm putting in downstairs. This is now my permanent address. This is my home."

Dani was sure Burke must be able to hear the pounding of her heart as it beat frantically against her chest. She placed her hands on his shoulders, hoping he wouldn't feel them shaking. "That's wonderful, Burke, but what about us?"

Burke groaned. "I'm making a muck of this, aren't I? I bought the damn house because I wanted to give us a place to live. I haven't bought any furniture or dishes or anything. I want us to pick them out together."

"I won't live with you, Burke. I have Patrick and Shamus to think about. Not to mention my own reputation." Dani was on a roll as her anger grew. She pulled out of his embrace and started pacing furiously. "Did you think buying a house would make any difference? If that's what you think of me, I don't want to see you again." She glared at him as she continued to pace. "I am not interested in your money."

Burke stopped her in her tracks with his roar. "Damn it, woman! I want to marry you. God only knows why, you jump to conclusions so fast. But there's no accounting for taste is there?" Burke thrust his hands through his hair in frustration, even as he took several deep breaths to calm himself.

"Marry me?" Dani asked in a small voice, almost afraid to repeat the question.

"Yes," he answered in exasperation. "I said so, didn't I?"

He only had a second to brace himself before she launched herself at him. Catching her in his strong arms, he held her close as she covered his face with kisses. His mouth, his cheeks, his nose, and everywhere else she could reach. He started to laugh. It was a deep rumble in his chest that she felt all the way to her heart.

"I take it this is a yes."

"Yes, yes, yes, yes, yes." She punctuated each answer with a kiss.

Burke whirled her around and around in circles until they were both dizzy. Then he collapsed on the floor, never once loosening his hold on her. She fell on top of him, and they rolled around on the floor, kissing and laughing until they were both out of breath. Dani ended up in the more comfortable position.

Burke was on the hard floor, but she was lying on top of him. It was a position she could easily get used to.

She lay there, content to just be in his arms until she had her breath back. Levering herself up, she rubbed her nose against his. "I'll have to remember to tell our children what a romantic proposal you made."

He sat up suddenly and plunked her on the floor next to him. Before she had a chance to complain about losing her soft bed, he reached inside his coat pocket and pulled out a small velvet box. "Well, I did have a different scenario in mind."

"Is it too late to get your version?" she asked shyly, feeling the heat creep up her cheeks and knowing she was blushing. It surprised her, and she tried to cover it by brushing her hair out of her face and straightening her clothing that had gone askew as they rolled around the floor.

Shifting his position so that he was kneeling in front of her, he laid the box in his lap, and then he took her left hand in his and brought it to his mouth. She felt his lips, warm and soft, on her fingers as he kissed them one by one. With his other hand, he tipped her chin up and looked into her eyes. His eyes were so dark and solemn as he held her gaze.

"Miss O'Rourke. You have my heart. I never thought I could ever love a woman, but you taught me I was wrong. I want you in my life forever. I want to share my life with you. Will you marry me?"

Dani's eye's widened. "You love me?"

"Yes," Burke answered.

"I love you, too. So very much." Framing his face with her hands, she held his gaze. "I never want to lose you. And I would be honored to marry you."

Burke wiped away a tear that clung to the corner of her eye as he bent down and touched his lips to hers. Slowly and softly at first and then harder as she kissed him back. Tumbling her onto her back, he kissed her urgently.

"I missed you so much," he muttered as he ran frantic kisses over her face and down her neck.

"I never want to be without you again." Running her fingers through his hair, she held him tighter.

His hands moved lovingly over her, touching her, as if reassuring himself that she was real and that she was his. His fingers quickly undid the buttons on her denim blouse and he flicked open the front clasp on her bra.

"So beautiful." Burke looked at her exposed flesh, and she could feel her breasts grow heavier under his heated gaze. "You're so beautiful," he whispered and her nipples tightened into dusky pink rosebuds, which ached with growing need.

Burke bent his head and ran his tongue around and around her nipple. His other hand was busy caressing and gently squeezing the other.

Dani moaned and gripped his shoulders tighter. She knew she wouldn't stop him this time. She loved him, and he loved her, and that was all that mattered.

Burke lapped at her nipple with his tongue and then began suckling on her. His mouth devoured her and she reveled in it. His hands roamed all over her body, over her back and down her thighs. He ran his palm up the front of her legs and gently inserted his hand between her legs in an unspoken plea.

Past all rational thought, she eagerly parted her legs. All she knew was that she wanted this man with every fiber of her being. She pulled his shirt out of his jeans and ran her hands over his chest, and when she found his nipples hidden in the thicket of male chest hair, she teased them with her fingers.

He stiffened and then suckled even harder at her breast. His hand continued to stroke between her legs, and Dani started to move her hips to the rhythm of his hand.

Shivering uncontrollably, she moaned and arched her hips toward him. She'd never felt anything like this in her life. She was burning with need, reaching for something she'd never experienced before.

"Burke, help me," she cried out, hardly knowing what she was saying.

Pulling his hand away, he quickly yanked open the button of her jeans and pulled down the zipper, before slipping his hand inside the opening. The minute his fingers touched her woman's softness, the feelings became even more intense.

Dani hardly knew what was happening to her. She cried out again as Burke touched her, stroking her heated flesh. All the feelings inside her exploded, and she held onto Burke for dear life, knowing instinctively he would keep her safe.

Burke held Dani as she shivered in his arms. He was so aroused it hurt to even breathe. But this was for Dani. For once in his life, someone else's satisfaction was more important than his own was. In fact, he found he took pleasure in her pleasure.

When Dani came back to her senses she moaned in embarrassment. "What are we doing? Anyone could come in and see us here. We're on the floor, for heaven's sake."

The blush that covered her face and slowly worked its way down over her breasts fascinated Burke. He hadn't known such a thing was even possible. "Lord, but you're precious," he said as he hugged her to him.

Dani was trying to straighten out her bra when she suddenly stopped. "But, you didn't...I mean..." she stammered.

Burke gently moved her hands and fastened her bra for her. "That's all right, love. I want our first time to be on our wedding night. You deserve it to be special. I just wanted to give you pleasure."

"You gave me great pleasure." Her sensual smile made his body throb and her words pleased him.

"I know," He returned her smile with a smug one of his own.

"Beast." She kissed him softly on the cheek.

"But you love me anyway," he replied. Her eyes were filled with love, and it was all for him as he fastened the buttons on her blouse and then he helped her to stand. "I still have a lot of money, you know."

"That was never really the problem," Dani answered. She toyed with the tail end of her shirt for a moment before dropping it and straightening it. She stood tall and proud as she met his questioning gaze. "It was the way I found out. Cynthia was smart enough to play on my insecurities, and I was foolish enough to let her. Once I'd had time to think about everything, I realized that you wouldn't have lied to me. But by then, you were gone."

Burke crossed his arms over his chest to keep from reaching for her to comfort her. "I'm sorry that I didn't tell you myself." He wanted her to understand his perspective. "You know why I didn't tell you at first." He raised his hand to stop her before she could speak. "But I should have told you later. For that I'm sorry. I never wanted to hurt you."

Bending down, he snagged the small box that had gotten lost in the midst of their passion. He turned to Dani and flipped open the lid, holding it out to her. In the box was a large solitary diamond that glittered in its golden setting.

"Do you like it? It reminded me of you, beautiful but without pretense." She stared at it for so long he began to get uncomfortable. "If you don't like it, we can exchange it."

"Not like it?" Her eyes were filled with longing when she finally looked at him. "It's the most beautiful ring I've ever seen." She held out her hand and waited.

Burke removed the ring from the box and slipped it onto Dani's finger before raising her hand to his mouth and kissing it to seal their vow. "I want the wedding next weekend. I can't wait any longer than that to make you mine."

"Next weekend," Dani squeaked. "How can we get so much done by next weekend? We need furniture. I need to rework some of my work schedule. What about the boys?" Dani tried to pull away, but he wouldn't relinquish his hold on her hand.

"The boys can come and live with us. You can keep the house on Peach Street for them or you can sell it to pay for their education. Whatever you want. We can buy furniture this week, and you can reschedule your customers." Burke wanted this all settled now. "Have I missed anything?"

"I need a dress and what about the minister and the church?" Dani's mind was obviously spinning with all the details. She looked a little dazed, but that was fine with him, because she had him to help her now. And he was very good with details. But seeing the look on her face, he relented, but only slightly.

"Two weeks, then. But that's it, I can't wait any longer than that." He knew he had to stand firm on this. He'd go mad if he had to wait any longer than that to make Dani his.

Seeing the frustration on his face, she finally took pity on him. "Two weeks. I promise I can do it in two weeks." Reaching up, she tugged his face down to receive her kiss. And what a kiss. Long and slow, it was filled with love and promise. "I don't want to wait either," she whispered when she finally released him.

"Good." He swallowed hard, trying to regain his equilibrium and ignore the pounding need of his body. Desperate for distraction, he changed the subject. "What do you think of the house? I bought it for us and for our family."

"I love this house. I was daydreaming about how I would furnish it when you came in." Dani laughed and spun around. "This will be our room and, Burke, I have so many ideas for the kitchen and living room."

She grabbed his hand and pulled him toward the stairs. "Come and tell me what you think of the living room arrangement that I have in mind."

Burke followed her down the stairs knowing that he would remember this moment for as long as he lived. Dani had given him his heart's desire and he would love and cherish her forever.

Chapter Sixteen

Burke held open the door of Jessie's Diner and ushered Dani inside. They had been busy all morning trying to make arrangements for their wedding, which was now only one week away. He'd made multimillion-dollar deals with less work then this event. But he didn't mind. Truth be told, he was having as much fun as Dani with the preparations, maybe even more.

Dani shot him a questioning look as they entered the warmth of the diner. "What's that smile for? You look incredibly smug about something."

"I was just thinking how much I enjoyed our morning."

Taking off her coat, she slipped into a booth next to the window. She waited until Burke had settled into the seat across from her before she spoke. "Thank you for taking such an active role in the wedding plans. I know that the groom is not usually expected to take such a large part in the planning. I guess it's just been harder on me than I expected it would be."

"What's been harder? What's wrong, Dani?" He was relieved that Dani had finally admitted that something was wrong. All week, he had sensed moments of sadness in her. Reaching across the table, he clasped her hand in his, holding it securely in his grasp. "You're not getting cold feet, are you?" He tried to make it sound like a joke, but it fell flat. He was afraid that maybe she was having second thoughts about their marriage.

"Oh, no, Burke. Never that." She squeezed his hand reassuringly. "I want to marry you more than anything else in the world."

"I figured that you did," he answered gruffly. "Then what is it, honey? What's been making you so sad?"

Sighing, she tugged her hand from his grasp and held out her left hand, staring at her engagement ring. "Sad. Yes, that's exactly what it is." She placed her hand flat on the table between them as she met his worried gaze. "It's just that when I pictured myself getting married, I always imagined my parents would be here too. I always dreamed that my mother would make my wedding dress and help me plan the reception. My father would walk me down the aisle and give me away. I never dreamed that they would both be gone." Her voice faded away, and her eyes had taken on a far-away look.

"I should have known you'd be thinking about your parents at a time like this." He placed his much larger hand over hers, hoping to give her some comfort. "But you've got Shamus and Patrick to give you away, and the three of us love you very much. We can't replace your parents, but everything will be okay. I promise."

"I know you're right. Most of the time I don't think about it, just sometimes." She pushed back the sleeves of her sweater and sat back in her seat. "Anyway, enough sadness. This is the happiest time in my life, and I intend to enjoy it."

"I don't mean to interrupt, but can I get you some coffee?"

They both looked up and saw Shannon, in her waitress uniform, standing next to their booth with menus in hand.

"You'll have to forgive us, Shannon." A smile grew on Dani's face as she spoke. "We were immersed in wedding plans."

"No problem." Shannon placed menus in front of them both and then slipped her order pad out of her uniform pocket. "Who's getting married?"

"Dani has agreed to marry me. Can you believe that a woman like Dani would agree to marry a guy like me? Some guys have all the luck." He no longer tried to hide his feelings for Dani. Instead, he wanted to shout to the world that she was his.

"Congratulations! When is the wedding?" Shannon reached over to hug Dani. She looked at Burke for a moment and then muttered, "what the heck", and leaned over and hugged him as well.

"Next Saturday," Dani replied. "We've been so busy this week, and I expect we'll be even busier next week." Scooping up the menus, she handed them back to Shannon who tucked them under her arm. "So you better bring me a large cup of coffee to keep up my strength. I'll also have the soup and sandwich special, please."

The waitress scribbled the order on her pad and then turned to Burke. "I'll have the same and a slice of apple pie if you have it. And Shannon, thanks for the congratulations and the hug."

"You're welcome." The other woman's face was covered in a bright red blush and a smile as she walked away.

They waited until they had their coffee in front of them before they resumed talking. "Okay." Dani pulled a large notebook from her purse as she spoke, laid it on the table, and opened it to where she had marked the page. Rummaging back in her purse, she hauled out a pen and then settled down to check her notes.

"We've invited a few close family friends to the ceremony. I've got my dress, and Patrick and Shamus have their tuxedos rented." She checked off the items as she listed them. "We've got to pick yours up at the cleaners this afternoon. I don't know anyone else who actually owns their own tuxedo," she teased.

Burke accepted the banter in good humor. Dani had taken every opportunity to tease him ever since she'd found out he had his own formal wear. "It's cost effective since I always had to attend some formal business function or another. Just be glad that I didn't donate it to charity when I moved."

"Yes, I'm sure it's very economical indeed. Not to mention that you look very dashing in it." Dani tried to keep a straight face and failed miserably. Her smile was wide as she went back to work on her list. "The church and license have been arranged. Flowers have been ordered. Work has been rescheduled." Stopping, she chewed on the end of her pen as she studied her list. "Can you think of anything we might have forgotten?"

"You're not sorry we're not having a reception, are you?" Burke asked.

"No, I'd rather wait until we get moved into our new home and have a house-warming party in a month or so instead." Dani flipped a page to consult yet another list. "If the wedding is under control, we need to worry about the house this week."

"We'll head to the paint shop after lunch and pick out the colors for the bedroom, bathroom, and kitchen. I think we should concentrate on those three rooms first. We can worry about the other rooms when we get moved in." Burke knew he had to keep a rein on Dani or she would be worn out by the time he got her to the altar. And that definitely wouldn't be good for the wedding night.

"I think you're probably right about that. We need to get some furniture for those rooms as well or we might end up sleeping on the floor on our wedding night." A pretty pink blush covered Dani's face as she finished speaking.

Burke knew she was remembering what happened on the bedroom floor the night he proposed to her. No, being on the floor wouldn't present too much of a problem at all. He knew what was running through Dani's mind because he had been having very similar thoughts. This last week had been murder on him. She was so beautiful, and he wanted her so badly. One more week, he consoled himself. One more week and she was his forever.

Shannon brought their lunch to the table, and they spent the next few minutes just eating. The homemade chicken noodle soup was steaming hot and delicious, and they devoured the meal in no time. Planning a wedding was hard work, and they were both starving. He had just finished his pie, and they were both sipping on their second cup of coffee when the door to the diner slammed open in a dramatic fashion.

There in the doorway stood Cynthia James, her face grim. She paused and looked around, homing in on Burke and Dani's table immediately. She sauntered forward.

"What does she want now?" Dani muttered.

"I have no idea," Burke answered, all the while wondering what new mischief the other woman wanted to make.

Marching up to the table, she shot Dani a dismissive look before turning and focusing her entire attention on Burke. "Can I speak to you in private, Burke?"

"We have nothing to discuss that needs privacy. If you have anything to say, say it here." Cynthia's voice had been soft and demure, which sent off warning bells in Burke's mind. Burke had learned from their one evening together that Cynthia loved an audience, and it seemed that she was about to put on a performance.

"Well," she continued in a small voice. "I don't think that this is something you'd want everyone to know." Cynthia looked pointedly at Dani as she said the word "everyone".

Burke sat back, crossed his arms over his chest, and waited.

Cynthia licked her lips and cleared her voice. "I heard that you and Dani were getting married, and I knew I couldn't let you do that to her." She gave Dani a look of pity as she continued on in a dramatic fashion. "I couldn't let him marry you like this. It's not fair to you."

The diner had grown considerably quieter as everyone pretended not to listen. Burke finally lost patience with waiting. It was time to go on the offensive. "You've got one minute to say what you came to say, and then Dani and I are leaving."

Cynthia shot him a hostile glare. "I don't think you'll be going anywhere real soon." She took a deep breath, aware that they now had the attention of everyone in the diner. "I'm pregnant."

Burke ignored the sudden whispers from the tables around them. "Congratulations," he replied evenly. "What has that got to do with either myself or Dani?"

Cynthia's face grew red with anger. "I'm carrying your baby, Burke." When that dramatic statement got no immediate response, she burst into tears. "How can you treat me and our child like that?" she wailed.

Burke noted cynically that while tears flowed down Cynthia's face, her mascara wasn't running. She had obviously made sure it was waterproof.

Ignoring the crying woman standing next to him, Burke turned his attention to the woman seated quietly across from him. Right now, he only had eyes for Dani. So much had happened between them. So much mistrust. He had to admit to himself, he had no idea how Dani would deal with this latest bit of mischief.

Dani met his gaze, and he knew she saw the love and the fear reflected there. Her own eyes widened, and he could tell the second she realized that he was more worried about her reaction than about Cynthia's announcement.

Dani studied Cynthia for a moment and then turned her attention back to him. Her simple nod let him know that she believed in him.

Assured of Dani's support, he turned his attention back to Cynthia, a hard gleam entering his eyes. "You may be pregnant, Cynthia, but it's not my child."

"How can you say that? After what happened on New Year's Eve." Drawing a handkerchief from her coat pocket, she dabbed at her tears. "How can you say that?"

Cynthia was trying hard to put just the right amount of tragic passion in her voice. Burke wondered if anyone else could hear the calculated tones underneath.

"New Year's Eve I left you at the country club, if you'll remember correctly."

"I know we had a small fight that night, but that doesn't matter now. I'm talking about before the dance." She held the wet hanky to her chest. "When you picked me up that night you told me how beautiful I was. How refined and unlike other women I was. And then later that night…" Cynthia paused for dramatic effect. "When you seduced me."

Burke couldn't help himself. He really tried, but he burst into laughter and applause. "What a performance, my dear. You really should go to Hollywood."

Cynthia stood there for a moment with a blank look on her face. Then she fixed a sad look on her face and turned to Dani. "How can you marry a monster who would desert his own child like this? How?"

Dani just shook her head in wonder. "Cynthia, I don't believe that you're carrying Burke's child. You may indeed be pregnant and, if you are, I hope you'll go talk to the baby's real father. Burke and I are still getting married."

Cynthia's face turned a mottled red. She obviously was past all caution at this point. "I'll make him pay. He owes me, and I'll make him pay."

Burke had finally had enough. "Cynthia, even if you are pregnant, any paternity test will show that I'm not the father. What are you hoping to gain by this little production? I can guarantee that even if you had succeeded in breaking off our wedding, I would have kept pursuing Dani. I would never turn to a woman like you. You're a self-centered, childish liar. You need to grow up, little girl. Why would I want you when I have a woman like Dani?"

"Go home." Burke kept his voice low and level. "You didn't get what you came for, and you're not going to. Just go home before you make a bigger fool of yourself than you already have."

Cynthia stood there for a moment, her whole body quivering in rage. Burke knew that she had expected Dani to throw her ring back at him and storm away. Then she, Cynthia, would console him. He would marry her and then she would have everything she ever wanted: money and status. Burke found himself feeling pity for her. She had no idea why her plan hadn't worked.

Cynthia struck back, trying to save face. "You're right. I'm not pregnant. I just thought I'd give you another chance to win me back. You're making the biggest mistake of your life by throwing me over for a little nobody like Dani O'Rourke. But it's your life. Don't come crying to me when you realize what a big mistake you've made. I won't take you back then. I'll be gone on to much bigger and better things than you."

Turning, she stormed out of the diner, aware that all eyes were on her. This time it was different. This time the eyes were not sympathetic, but hostile. She pushed open the door of the diner and ran down the sidewalk.

Silence. The silence in the diner was deafening. Burke slowly stood and faced the rest of the people who were dining there. "I'm sorry you had your meal interrupted."

Picking up Dani's coat from the seat, he waited as she stood. Dani quietly slipped on her coat and grabbed her purse. He motioned to Shannon, and she hurried over from the counter from where she had watched the entire scene. Her eyes were huge as he handed her several bills. "This should cover our lunch."

"Oh yes, and more. Wait and I'll get you your change."

"Keep the change." Placing his hand on the small of Dani's back, he lead her urged her toward the door.

Mrs. Woods, who had been seated at a table by the door, started to clap. A chair scraped back as another patron stood and also started to clap. More chairs scraped, and a second later, the room was filled with applause and congratulations as a smiling Burke ushered his blushing bride-to-be out of the diner.

Chapter Seventeen

"I didn't think I'd ever get you alone." Sweeping her into his arms, Burke nudged open the door with his elbow and carried her through the front door of their new home.

Dani tightened her arms around his neck. "It was a lovely surprise, don't you think? I really didn't expect Patrick and Shamus to plan a surprise reception. I didn't suspect a thing."

"The reception at your house was great, but I didn't think we'd ever be able to get away from all your friends and neighbors. Now that you're mine, I don't want to share you. At least not tonight." Burke tightened his grip on Dani as he headed up the stairs.

"It's wonderful to be home." And she was home, she thought as she rested her head on his strong shoulder. The last two weeks had been a whirlwind of activity, getting the house ready to move into and planning the wedding.

Burke entered the master bedroom and slowly lowered her until her feet were touching the floor. "Did I tell you how beautiful you look?"

She peered at herself in the mirror, meeting Burke's eyes as he gazed at her reflection. She knew that Burke thought that she looked like an angel, with her long hair flowing to her waist and a gown of white lace and satin hugging her body. At least that's what he told her earlier, and she knew she would always treasure the compliment. She loved the dress, which was not a traditional long one with a train, but a three-quarter length one with long sleeves and a high collar and a long row of small pearl buttons running from the top of the collar to the tip of the hem.

Dani saw the heated look in Burke's eyes and couldn't stop herself from blushing with pleasure. "Thank you. You look beautiful too. Well, handsome anyway." And he did look wonderful in a black tuxedo. It made him look even bigger and better looking that usual, if such a thing was possible.

"Do you want me to help you undo your dress? There's an awful lot of buttons," Burke's breath teased her skin as he leaned down to whisper in her ear. He placed a soft kiss on the side of her neck, his gaze still holding hers in the mirror.

Her mouth was suddenly very dry, and she licked her lips in a nervous gesture. "No." Her hand drifted up to the buttons at her neck. "I can do it myself."

"Hey," Placing his hand under her chin, he tilted her face up so that she was looking at him. "There's nothing to be afraid of, Dani. You're safe with me. I'll never do anything you don't want me to, and I won't rush you. We have all night together, and all the nights for the rest of our life."

"I know it's silly to be nervous, but I can't seem to help myself." She took a deep breath, hoping he would understand.

"It's not silly, honey, it's natural. Why don't you go and change in the bathroom, and I'll go get us some champagne from the kitchen. Okay?"

"Okay." She watched as Burke left the room, and then she picked up her small bag that she had left there yesterday and hurried to the bathroom to change.

As she started to undress, Dani's thoughts drifted back over the last two weeks. She had been so busy right up until the ceremony late this afternoon that she supposed she hadn't had time to be nervous. She looked at the gold band that she now wore nestled on her left hand next to her engagement ring and smiled. She could hardly believe that they were really married.

The ceremony had been simple, but lovely, and had been held in the chapel at the United Church of Jamesville. It had been planned as a small gathering with Patrick, Shamus, and a few close friends as witnesses. But about ten minutes before they were to start, other people had begun to show up. Some, neighbors from her street, and others, people she had done work for.

Dani had been surprised after the ceremony, when Patrick and Shamus had ushered all their neighbors and friends back to their house on Peach Street for a buffet reception. Everyone had brought something along to the reception, so there had been no shortage of good food to eat. Mrs. Woods had made several of her blue-ribbon winning pies. But the biggest surprise came from Mr. Carter and his wife who had even had a wedding cake made special for them. It was a three-tiered confection of white with candy roses and blue icing ribbons. She had been deeply touched to by people's good wishes for her and Burke.

The walk down the aisle at the church had filled her with joy. Patrick and Shamus had seemed so proud as they both gave her away. They'd looked so handsome in their tuxedos, and she realized that they were almost grown men now. She had seen Patrick talking seriously to Burke before the ceremony and wondered if Patrick had given Burke the traditional fatherly lecture. The thought made her giggle.

When she finished removing her wedding dress, she hung it on the back of the door, before slipping into a long pale blue nightgown that flowed around her legs and was cut quite low in the front. She slipped the matching robe over it and tied it under her breasts. *I look like a bride*, she thought as she stared at herself in the mirror. She had a glow about her that she knew love had put there.

A tap at the door made her start.

"Dani, honey, are you all right?"

Burke sounded worried. She must have been longer than she thought. Taking a deep breath, she opened the bathroom door.

Burke opened his mouth to speak and then quickly snapped it shut. He just stood there and stared at her. His gaze started at the top of her head and flowed down her body, slowing on her face and stopping for a moment at her breasts before continuing down to her feet, and back up to her face again. He said nothing. In fact, he stared so long that she started to fidget, slightly uncomfortable, yet pleased by his reaction.

"My God, you're lovely," His eyes caressed her as he spoke. Burke held out his hand to her, and she placed her smaller hand in his, showing him without words that she trusted him.

Bringing her hand to his lips, he kissed her fingers one at a time. Keeping hold of her hand, he led her back to their bedroom. Slowly, he untied the ribbons of her robe and gently slipped it from her shoulders. Neither of them paid attention to it as it drifted to the floor.

Burke never took his eyes off her face as he reached for her, lifted her into his arms, and carried her over to the bed. The bed was an antique sleigh bed that he had purchased as a wedding gift for her last week when she had admired it in an antique shop. Tonight, it was her wedding bed.

He lowered her onto the turned-back covers and then tucked them around her. Picking up a champagne glass from the table next to the bed, he had a sip of the golden liquid before handing the glass to her.

Burke stood back from the bed and slipped out of his shirt. His socks, pants and underwear quickly followed. When he was naked, he slipped into bed next to her.

Dani sipped nervously at the champagne as she watched him disrobe. The glass in her hand trembled. "I don't know what's wrong with me."

Burke carefully removed the glass from her hand and placed it back on the bedside table. "It's all right, love," he whispered softly in her ear and then ran light kisses down the side of her neck.

Sighing at his touch, she forgot about being nervous as his lips ran up the curve of her neck and lightly touched her lips. Ever so gently, his lips nibbled at hers until it wasn't enough. Dani wanted more of his touch. Using her tongue, she licked at his lips. The kiss started soft and sweet and slowly became something harder and deeper as their need for each other grew. His lips devoured hers, tasting and savoring. Then his tongue delved into her mouth, exploring and claiming the territory as his own.

His hands had been just as busy as his mouth, and Dani suddenly realized that her breasts were bare, her nightgown slipped down to her waist.

He slid his fingers over her skin, testing its softness, relearning its textures before he covered her breasts with his hands, his thumbs brushing her nipples. They puckered and tightened as he continued to stroke them.

Pulling his mouth from hers, he kissed a heated path down her neck to her breasts. He drew one nipple into his mouth and sucked gently on it. Desire thrummed through her body, and she cried out, pulling his head tight to her. Burke muttered his approval and proceeded to give her other breast the same treatment.

"You're so perfect for me. You were made for me." Burke whispered as he moved from one breast to the other.

Dani just moaned in agreement. She couldn't speak if her life depended on it. Her hands stroked over his back. She loved to touch him, his skin was so firm and warm, and the muscles underneath rippled when he moved.

Burke pulled back from her and admired her as she lay there on the bed. His eyes smoldered as he tugged the nightgown down over her hips. She lifted her bottom off the bed so he could remove the garment. With the bed covers pushed back, he looked at her, seeing all of her for the first time.

Dani began to feel self-conscious and started to cover herself with the sheet. The barest touch of his hand on her arm stopped her.

"Let me look at you, love. You're so beautiful."

Opening her hand, she let go her grip on the sheet, and it slid back down the pool at her waist. She let him draw it the rest of the way down until she was exposed again. She was so caught up in her own embarrassment that it took her a moment to realize that he was naked, too.

For the first time, she really looked at him, and he stole her breath away. He was so strong and hard, yet his skin was supple and smooth. His chest had a thick covering of dark hair that narrowed down his stomach. Dani followed the arrow down with her eyes.

"Oh my." She glanced up to see Burke's amused gaze on hers. "You're much bigger then I imagined. I mean, you're a big man...I mean tall...I just never thought..." Dani looked at him helplessly.

"Don't worry, sweetheart." His voice was tender and amused. "We'll be perfect together. We were made for each other." Reaching out, he drew her hand to him, pressing her fingers against his erection. "Go ahead and touch me. Feel what you do to me."

Dani tentatively touched him. "Your skin is so soft," she exclaimed as she ran her fingers gently up and down his hard length. Slowly, she circled him with her hand and moved up and down, fascinated by the texture and by his response, for Burke was absolutely rigid, every muscle tense.

He endured the tender torture for a few moments before he removed her hand from him. Before she had time to protest, he swooped down and took her mouth in another searing kiss. Like a man possessed, he moved his hands over her body, touching and exploring every inch of her. He found the nest of curls between her thighs, and she moaned when he gently parted her. His fingers moved over her heated skin, around and around until her hips started to move. He slid one of his long, thick fingers into her wet warmth, testing her readiness.

Dani moved her hips as Burke continued to tease and touched her. She couldn't help herself. "Now. I want you, now." Clutching at his shoulders, she tried to pull him closer to her.

"Yes," he groaned as he guided himself to her opening.

When he started to enter her, she tensed and pulled back slightly. It hurt a little as he tried to forge a path inside her.

"You're so tight. Just relax, and let me in." Burke was breathing hard as he spoke.

She took a deep breath and slowly released it. As her body relaxed, he slipped a little bit deeper inside her. Unable to wait any longer, she lifted her hips toward him, and at the same time, she gripped his butt and pulled him downward. He was past her body's barrier before he even realized it. Dani gasped at the slight pain and the uncomfortable feeling of fullness, but she held on tight to him, wanting him all the way inside her.

"It's okay now, it's okay." He held himself still, obviously trying to keep himself in check. She slid her hands up his back, his hard flesh slick beneath her palms. Her fingers dug into his shoulders, and still he didn't move.

Dani shifted her body slightly to try and accommodate him, when Burke's control finally snapped. She was just getting used to the full feeling of having him inside her when she felt the change in him. When he started to pull away, she feared that he was trying to leave her, and she tried to pull him back. Instead, he surged into her again. Soon she was caught up in the rhythm as he plunged in and out, faster and faster. Wrapping her legs around his hips, she hung on tight.

She was reaching for that wonderful pleasure he had given her before. She was so close. Burke reached between their bodies and touched her, stroking her nub of desire. That was all it took. Dani felt herself explode with pleasure.

As soon as she cried out, Burke drove himself deep one final time and emptied himself into her. Her inner muscles clamped down hard around him as he yelled out his release. His arms tightened round her before he groaned and collapsed onto the bed next to her. It took a few long minutes before he found his voice to speak.

"Are you okay, honey?" Levering himself up onto his elbows, he stared down at her.

The slight movement pushed him deeper and she couldn't suppress a moan of desire. He felt so good inside her.

"Dani, did I hurt you?" He carefully pulled out of her and rolled onto his back, cradling her in his arms. "Look at me, love," he commanded softly.

"Hmmm," Dani answered as she snuggled her face against his chest.

Burke's hands moved in a soothing rhythm up and down her back. "I'm sorry if I hurt you, love."

Dani slowly looked up, opened her eyes, and smiled. "You didn't hurt me. I may never move again, but you didn't hurt me."

His look of concern quickly became one of satisfaction. "Wore you out, did I?"

Dani didn't mind if he looked a little smug. "It was wonderful. More than I had even imagined it would be. When can we do it again?" She gave him a mischievous little grin.

He laughed. "I've created a monster. You'll have to give me a few minutes."

"Wore you out, did I?" Dani asked smugly.

Burke pounced on her and kissed her soundly as they rolled around in the big bed. "I'll teach you to tease me," he growled.

A long while later, Dani was recovering from the pleasure of making love once again. She snuggled contentedly next to Burke's large body. "I guess you taught me a lesson," she yawned sleepily. "Will you teach me more later?"

"We'll teach each other, love, we'll teach each other." Burke gathered the already sleeping Dani into his arms and held her close to his heart. As he drifted off to sleep, it occurred to him that she hadn't even seemed to notice the disfiguring scar on his leg. His arms closed even tighter around the treasure he had been lucky enough to find. She was his now, forever.

Epilogue

"This is not how I imagined I'd spend the first morning of my wedded life." Her grumble was half-hearted as she ambled along next to Burke.

"You're not up to any bedroom activities this morning, Mrs. Black," he teased her. "I didn't want to hurt you, Dani. You have to give yourself time to recover," he added more seriously.

"I know." She knew he had wanted her as soon as they awoke this morning, but had held back in concern for her. "I just love you so much."

"I love you too, Dani, and we've got all the mornings of our life ahead of us."

They crunched through the snow, hand in hand, as they explored the land surrounding their home. They had spent so much time in the last two weeks getting the house habitable that they hadn't really had time for the outside.

"I can't wait to start a garden this spring." She loved the big white farmhouse with all the land surrounding it. The house had included the ten acres surrounding it, and Dani was looking forward to spending many an hour just rambling around the place.

She was more than ready to start their life together, but there was one thing left that bothered her slightly. "Do you think we'll have any more trouble with Cynthia?"

"Where did that come from?" Burke stopped dead in his tracks. "You're not worried about her, are you?"

"Not worried, exactly. I just hope she's finished with all her little tricks for good. I'd just like to get on with life and not have to worry about what she's going to do next." Dani scuffed her boot in the snow as she spoke.

"You don't have to worry about her anymore, Dani," Burke said. "If I'd known this was on your mind, I could have told you about Cynthia sooner."

"What about Cynthia?" Dani questioned. "What's she done now?"

"I went to see her."

"You did!" She hadn't expected this. "You didn't tell me that."

"Because I didn't want you to worry. Listen to me, Dani. I didn't even speak to her. She wasn't there."

"What were you going to say to her?"

"I was merely going to inform her that if she pulled another stunt like the last one she'd find herself in court facing charges of slander. Then there's also the business of how she found out about the money I loaned you. She had to have gotten that from someone who worked at the bank."

"I never thought about that," Dani admitted as they resumed walking.

"I did. So I talked to her father instead. As the bank's president, he understood what the consequences would be if

212

anything like this ever happened again." Burke thought for a moment before continuing. "Your goodness must be rubbing off on me, because I told him I didn't want him to investigate how Cynthia found out that information. It's over, with no real harm done."

Dani pulled him into a big hug. "I'm glad. I just want to put it all behind us now." She hesitated for a moment. "Cynthia came to see me."

"She what!" Burke exploded just as Dani had known he would. "What did she want?"

She captured Burke's face in her hands and went up on her toes so she could kiss him. He wasn't distracted. His face was still dark with anger. Sighing, she released him.

"Believe it or not, she came to apologize." Burke gave her a look that clearly said he didn't believe her, but Dani forged ahead. "I think it was genuine. After the scene in the diner, a lot of people let her know what they thought of her actions. I got the feeling that for the first time in her life, Cynthia understands that there are consequences for her actions."

Dani started walking again, and Burke reluctantly fell into step beside her. His hand reached out to hold hers, and she felt a great relief at finally having that out in the open. "Cynthia promised we have nothing to worry about from now on. She wished us well before she left the house."

"It doesn't matter. Cynthia has left town. She's gone to stay with an aunt in Vermont." Burke let that little bit of information just slip out as if it were insignificant.

Dani was genuinely shocked. "I didn't think she would ever leave Jamesville. I could tell she was having a hard time handling the fallout from the incident in the diner, but it never occurred to me that she'd actually leave her home." Dani felt sorry for Cynthia, but at the same time she was looking forward to some peace and quiet for her and Burke for a change.

"I don't think we'll have to worry about Cynthia causing any more trouble." Burke leaned down and planted a quick kiss on her mouth, effectively closing that subject for the time being. "Speaking of the future, have you decided what you're going to do about work? You don't have to work if you don't want to."

She knew he was treading carefully here, not knowing how she'd react to such a suggestion. "Do you want me to stop working?"

"Not if you don't want to. I just want you to be happy."

"I've got to think about things a little more. There's been so much happening lately that I haven't really had time to think past the wedding." She stopped and looked out over the snow covered ground. "How do you feel about kids? We didn't use any protection last night."

"I'd love to have a baby, but only when you're ready."

"Hmm," Dani answered as she continued walking. "But if I worked at home, that would make having babies much easier."

"Dani, what are you talking about? And what about having a baby?" Burke tugged on her hand until she stopped. The frustration on his face was obvious, so she took pity on him.

"I could set up a small place next to my desk for the baby, don't you think? Then the baby could come to work with me everyday." Dani smiled at the thought of a dark-haired baby. "I think it will work perfectly."

"You want a baby. Immediately." He waited as she nodded her agreement. Unable to contain himself, he picked her up and twirled her around. "Thank you, Dani. You don't know how much this means to me." He put her back down but didn't let her go. "There's just one thing."

"What?"

"What did you mean about working at home?"

"Oh, that. Well, I'm going to write books like I've always dreamed of. I can do that for a few hours every day so we'll still have lots of time for all the babies and us. I've got some money saved so we won't starve. What do you think?"

"I think it's a wonderful idea." Burke hesitated for a moment. "Save your money for a rainy day. I think it's time you let someone help you for a change. Besides, I don't doubt that you'll be successful, even if it takes a while." He looked thoughtful for a moment. "You know, there was a business associate in Chicago whose wife worked in publishing."

Dani laughed and hugged him "Thank you, but this is something I need to do on my own." She loved him all the more for his support.

"Besides, you're busy with your work, and with Patrick and Shamus moving in with us today, I can guarantee that our home will be filled with chaos. I'll have to finish up all my scheduled work, and then I'm going to retire from my cleaning business."

Burke looked solemn. "How do you feel about that? I know what it's like to change careers. It can be exhilarating and scary all at once."

Dani's heart filled with love, and she reached out and placed her hand on his chest. Her wedding rings gleamed in the morning sun. "I know I'll be all right, because we're together."

"Together," Burke murmured as he reached down to kiss her. It was a long time before he let her go.

"Let's go home." Dani pulled Burke back up the driveway. "I'm feeling much better now, after a brisk morning walk. I may need a nap this afternoon though. Want to join me?" she asked coyly.

"I think that maybe a nap is a real good idea." Burke smiled as he walked toward the house with Dani tucked safely under his arm. This beautiful woman had made his life complete. The future was no longer black. His world was now full of light.

N. J. Walters

N.J. Walters has always been a voracious reader of romance novels and decided one day that she could write one as well. The contemporary story, Discovering Dani, was the very first novel she wrote while living in a little town much like the one Dani O'Rourke lives in, though all other similarities to Dani's life pretty much end there. Then she wrote another one that followed up on Dani's friends and neighbors. But she didn't consider herself a "real" writer yet.

Just a few years later N. J. had a mid-life crisis at a fairly young age, gave notice after ten years at her job on a Friday and received a tentative acceptance for her first published novel (an erotic romance) from a publisher on the following Sunday.

Happily married for over eighteen years to the love of her life, with his encouragement and support she gave up the job of selling books for the more pleasurable job of writing them. She now spends her days writing, reading and reviewing books. It's a tough life, but someone's got to do it. And some days she actually feels like a "real" writer.

N.J. enjoys hearing from readers, and she can be reached at njwalters22@yahoo.ca. You can check out her web site at www.njwalters.com.

Printed in the United States
59253LVS00002BA/136